BEAR

SHADOWRIDGE GUARDIANS MC

BECCA JAMESON

PHOTOGRAPHY BY
FURIOUS FOTOG

COVER MODEL
TONY BRETTMAN

ABOUT SHADOWRIDGE GUARDIANS MC

Combining the sizzling talents of bestselling authors Pepper North, Kate Oliver, and Becca Jameson, the Shadowridge Guardians are guaranteed to give you a thrill and leave you dreaming of your own throbbing motorcycle joyride.

Are you daring enough to ride with a club of rough, growly, commanding men? The protective Daddies of the Shadowridge Guardians Motorcycle Club will stop at nothing to ensure the safety and protection of everything that belongs to them: their Littles, their club, and their town. Throw in some sassy, naughty, mischievous women who won't hesitate to serve their fair share of attitude even in the face of looming danger, and this brand new MC Romance series is ready to ignite!

Shadowridge Guardians MC
Steele by Pepper North
Kade by Kate Oliver
Atlas by Becca Jameson
Doc by Kate Oliver
Gabriel by Becca Jameson

Talon by Pepper North
Bear by Becca Jameson
Faust by Pepper North
Storm by Kate Oliver
Blade by Pepper North
King by Kate Oliver
Rock by Becca Jameson

"Angel, you might want to rethink whatever's brewing in that pretty head of yours..."

Adelaine has left her old life behind and started fresh. She's happy. She has new friends, a new job, and far less stress. Nothing can burst her bubble. Until it does. When the fiancé she left at the altar walks through the door of the body shop where she works, all the blood drains from her face.

Bear has at least as many secrets as Addie. He doesn't care that he's mysterious. What he does care about is protecting the Littles in his MC, and with his size, this is not an issue. If anyone dares mess with the women in the club, they will find themselves on the receiving end of his wrath. If anyone dares mess with the angel who has recently stolen his heart though...

Stepping in as Addie's personal protection detail is a no brainer, but guarding his heart is nearly impossible.

PROLOGUE

"Adelaine! What are you doing? Why isn't your dress on?"

Addie cringed at the shrill tone of her mother's voice. She closed her eyes and took a deep breath. *You can do this. You can do this.*

I can't do this.

The clack of her mother's shoes hurrying across the floor made Addie wince.

"Good grief. The guests are in their seats, the groomsmen are lined up at the altar, and you're standing here in your lingerie."

Addie bit her tongue. It wouldn't do any good to speak. It would be better if she just let her mother roll right over her— as usual.

"Arms up. Seriously, Adelaine. I don't understand you sometimes—and where are your bridesmaids? If you were more pleasant, they would be in here helping you." The pitch of her mother's voice rose with each sentence, grating on Addie's last nerve.

Like a robot, she held out her arms and let her mother lower the ugly wedding dress down her body. It was hideous.

Addie never would have chosen anything like it for herself. All sleek body-fitting satin that wrapped tightly around her, making her look like a hooker in her opinion.

And the bridesmaids? Ha. Addie didn't even know half their names. They were the daughters of her mother's friends and the girlfriends of her fiancé's groomsmen. She didn't know any of them. That's why they weren't in the bride's room, helping her get dressed. Why would they be?

"Suck your stomach in, Adelaine," her mother ordered as she worked the zipper up the back of the ugliest wedding dress known to mankind.

When Addie let herself look in the mirror, she saw a Barbie. Her long hair was nearly black and styled to perfection in a poufed updo that she'd had no say in. Tendrils of it hung in perfect ringlets that had been shellacked to the point that she doubted she'd ever get all the hairspray out of it.

Her skin was pale—much to her mother's dismay—because she'd been born this way and had refused to get a spray tan for her mother's special day. Honestly, Addie didn't even recognize herself. Who was this woman staring back at her? The makeup artist had applied long fake lashes and a year's worth of eyeshadow. The woman had spent the entire two hours grumbling under her breath about not having a foundation as pale as Addie's skin.

"Pull your shoulders back. You look like you're heading to your death instead of the altar. This is the most important day of your life, Adelaine. Stand tall. Smile. Try not to make me look bad. The room is filled with my most important clients."

Heaven forbid if Caroline Albrecht's clients weren't wowed by this most important business deal.

And that's what her wedding was—a business deal. Addie was being married off to the son of one of Caroline's business associates.

Joseph Bulgari. Such a pretentious ass. The man had never

once called Adelaine by her preferred nickname, even though she'd told him to call her Addie every time she'd seen him.

And how many times had that been? Twelve. That's how many times Addie had been in the presence of her future husband, and the future was now. Today. This hour.

The door to the bride's room opened again, and Addie looked up to see the wedding planner stick her head inside. "They're ready for you, Mrs. Albrecht." The woman was speaking to Addie's mother. Her *mother*! Not one person gathered at this church today cared a single bit about Addie herself —the bride.

Caroline sighed. "I've done the best I can with you. Please don't embarrass me." She turned and clacked out of the room on her heels.

Addie stared for a moment longer at her reflection before she used the mirror to glance toward the door her mother had just exited through. Thank God she'd shut the door. Addie could hear the faint sounds of the prelude and knew she had only a minute before she would be expected at the altar.

She would be walking herself down the aisle because her father had passed away five years ago, she had no brothers or uncles, and her mother preferred to be seated before Addie entered.

The wedding was all arranged. Every moment of this day had been organized and planned by Caroline Albrecht, Joseph Bulgari Sr., and his wife Marilyn.

Addie's heart raced as she turned around. She glanced around the room before her gaze landed on her suitcases and oversized purse. She had no idea what was in those suitcases —her mother had packed them—but she did know what was in her purse because she'd added several things to it herself.

Next to those three pieces of luggage was a door that led to the back hallway of the church and the side entrance. It was the door she'd used to enter the church hours ago so that no one would get a glimpse of her.

Addie looked toward the door the wedding planner would undoubtedly come through again in less than a minute.

Breathing deeply, Addie made her decision. She bent down, tugged off her heels, tossed them aside, and raced toward her luggage. In seconds, she had her bag over her shoulder and a suitcase in each hand. She pushed through the door.

She could hear the prelude still playing. No one was in the hallway. She turned toward the exit, dragging the brand-new suitcases with their perfectly functioning wheels, and slammed her hip into the bar across the door leading to freedom.

When it opened, she burst into the sunlight and glanced around. *Now what?*

There was a row of cars along the curb on this side of the church. Four of them were limos with drivers standing at the ready. All four men looked toward Addie, eyes wide.

Please, for the love of all that is holy, let them take pity on me.

Addie knew she looked like a madwoman running down the sidewalk toward the limos. She had bare feet, two large suitcases, and a giant pink purse that matched nothing.

"Which one of you is going to take me away from here?" she begged as she approached.

"Uh... Ma'am? Aren't you supposed to be getting married?" one older man asked.

"Not today," Addie answered. "Who's going to drive?" She glanced over her shoulder, certain she would be caught at any moment. "Please. This is important. Do any of you have a daughter?" There. She would appeal to their fatherly senses.

"Yes," the driver of the second limo, a younger man, tentatively responded.

"Would you marry her off to a man she barely knows just to improve your family's standing in society?"

"No," he muttered.

She rushed toward him as if it were decided. *Please, let it be decided.*

When he didn't move, she opened the driver's door, reached in, and popped the trunk. He could either help her, or she would take his limo.

"Ma'am?" the younger driver said louder. "Are you sure about this?"

"Shit," the older gentleman mumbled. "Her mother will fire all of us."

Addie ignored them as she dragged her suitcases to the trunk of the younger driver's limo. She was in a panic as she worked to lift the first one. It was fucking heavy. She was going to have to leave them behind.

Giving up, she tugged up her skirt and hurried back to the open driver's door. With one more glance at the young man who owned this limo, she said, "Either you're driving, or I am."

He jogged toward her and opened the back door. "Fuck," he muttered. "Get in." He looked over his shoulder. "James, get her luggage, will you?"

Addie held her breath as she watched the driver of the third limo run over and load her things in the trunk.

As soon as her own driver was in his seat with the door closed, she ordered, "*Go.*"

"I'm going to lose my job," he grumbled as he pulled away from the curb.

Addie looked over her shoulder out the window to find the wedding planner standing on the sidewalk, looking around. When the woman spotted the limo driving away, her eyes went huge, and she started running toward Addie's getaway car, waving her hands.

That woman was going to get fired, too. Addie didn't care. She didn't even know the woman's name. She didn't think the woman had ever looked her in the eye or addressed her directly, nor had Addie been specifically introduced to the woman who'd planned this entire farce. Addie didn't give a shit if the woman got fired. Served her right.

Addie finally began to calm down as soon as the driver pulled around the corner.

"Ma'am, what's your plan?"

Addie chewed on her bottom lip, thinking. Finally, she met his gaze in the rearview mirror. "Please take me to the nearest bank so I can make a withdrawal. After that, I'd like to go to the airport. I'll give you a handsome tip if you promise to do those two things for me. You're a good man. I'm sorry if you get fired. When you tuck your daughter into bed tonight, remember she's a human being who deserves to make her own choices in life."

"Yes, ma'am."

"Addie. My name is Addie."

"Addie." He smiled at her in the rearview mirror. There were tears in his eyes. "I'm sorry for whatever you're dealing with, Addie."

"Me, too." She sighed.

"Where will you go?"

"I don't know. Wherever the first flight out is headed." That was the extent of her plan, but it was a start.

Adelaine Albrecht was reclaiming her life, starting now.

CHAPTER
ONE

"Can you make extra pancakes this morning, Bear?"

Bear glanced over his shoulder at Eden, the bubbly Little who'd bounded into the room with far more energy than usual. He lifted his brow at Gabriel, her Daddy, as he followed her into the kitchen wearing a smirk.

"Do you have two stomachs this morning, Little one?" he asked Eden as he returned his attention to flipping pancakes.

She giggled. "No, silly. I want to take a plate out to my friend Addie."

"Who's Addie," Bear asked as he filled a plate and set it in front of Eden.

Eden grinned up at him. "My friend from the university. She's in my algebra class. She got a job as the receptionist, working for Kade in the motorcycle shop. It's her first day, so I thought it would be good hospitality to bring her some pancakes."

Bear grunted. "Sure." He didn't mind making extra pancakes, nor did he mind listening to Eden ramble on about her friend. "Is she Little? Do you want my special bear-shaped pancakes with chocolate chips for the eyes, nose, and mouth? Or just regular pancakes?"

Eden lit up. "Oh. Mmm. I don't really know yet if she's Little. She might be. But either way, who doesn't like bear pancakes? You don't have to be Little to eat pretty food."

Bear narrowed his gaze at her, trying not to chuckle and failing. "Not sure I like the idea of you calling my food pretty."

The Little imp giggled before she cut a huge bite and stuffed it in her mouth.

"Eden," Gabriel warned, "smaller bites and chew your food. You're not in a hurry. Addie doesn't even start her shift until nine, and remember what I told you. You may go out and say hello. You may also bring her pancakes, but you may not stay and bother her."

"Yes, Sir," Eden muttered.

Bear turned back around to hide his expression. The Little girl was already on the path toward a spanking, and the sun was barely up. He couldn't keep the smile from his face.

Bear was happy for his brothers. So many of them had met the perfect women who completed them and made their lives fuller and richer. The clubhouse was a hell of a lot more interesting with the addition of giggles and shenanigans. It warmed his heart.

Considering the fact that Bear would never find and claim a Little of his own, it was nice to be able to cook breakfast for everyone else's Littles most days and listen to their banter and planned antics. He lived vicariously through his brothers, the Daddies of the Shadowridge Guardians MC.

In addition, Bear often found himself playing the role of babysitter, especially in the mornings when his brothers sometimes needed to get to work before their Littles were ready to start their days. He grumbled good-naturedly about his "duties" sometimes, but it was all a façade. He secretly loved spending time with each and every one of them, and his brothers knew it.

Bear concentrated on making three of his specialty bear pancakes before sliding them onto a plate. He put syrup in a small plastic container with a lid and added it, along with a fork and knife, to the pancakes before placing a domed lid over the top.

"Oh, that's perfect," Eden declared when Bear set it on the table. "Thank you so much."

"Tell your friend to just leave the plate and silverware behind the counter. I'll go out in a while and collect it."

Eden jumped up from her chair. "Can we go now, Daddy?" she asked Gabriel.

Gabriel laughed. "After I finish my coffee. Go brush your teeth."

When Eden took off skipping away from the kitchen, Gabriel and Bear called after her at the same time, "No running!"

Gabriel groaned as she disappeared. "You'd think after spraining her ankle and spending time in Doc's office as well as urgent care, she would stop running in the house."

Bear smirked. "I'm pretty sure I'd faint if I didn't have to yell at one of them for running before breakfast was even over. I'm equally certain they enjoy antagonizing us first thing in the morning. It sets a tone."

Gabriel laughed. "If by tone you mean a shade of pink or red on half their bottoms, you're right."

Bear sat across from Gabriel, joining him with a mug of coffee. Any minute now, he would need to prepare more plates of food, but it was quiet during this lull. "Have you met this friend Eden is so excited about?"

"Yes. They've had a few study sessions together. Once at the library on the university campus and once at the coffee shop nearby."

Bear chuckled. "I guess you didn't let Eden go alone."

"Fuck no. I'm still not ready to let her out of my sight. Even though Rat is in jail and the rest of the Devil's Jesters seem to be staying in their own town lately, I don't trust any of them."

Bear nodded. "I can understand that. I wouldn't either if I

were in your shoes." Bear had felt every bit of the angst a few of his brothers had experienced dealing with the Devil's Jesters and the problems they'd caused for both Eden and Talon's Little girl, Elizabeth. The entire town would appreciate it if the Jesters stayed away.

Gabriel pushed to standing. "I guess I better take Eden out to the shop. She's so excited that she was able to get Adelaine an interview and a job. Apparently, her friend is only taking a few classes a semester because she has to work full-time to afford the tuition and her expenses."

Bear cringed. "I hate that for her. Do you think Kade is paying her enough to help her stay afloat?" It bothered Bear when women were on their own, trying to make ends meet. It sounded like that was the case with Adelaine.

He'd do a bit of snooping later today and make sure she was above water. If she was important to Eden, he'd make her important to him, too, though he had no idea what he might do if the woman was strapped for cash. It wasn't as though he could pay her rent or cover her tuition without her knowing. Or hell, maybe he could…

In any case, he was getting ahead of himself. Maybe she was fine. Maybe she had parents who were helping her out, and Eden didn't know that about her.

As Gabriel set his mug in the dishwasher, Talon and Elizabeth entered the kitchen, followed by Faust and Storm. It was time to flip some more pancakes.

CHAPTER
TWO

Addie was nervous when she arrived at the Shadowridge Guardians MC fifteen minutes before nine. She wasn't sure where to park her car, as there seemed to be a lot of cars around the entrance. So she parked it in the street, checked all around to make sure there wasn't a fire hydrant or a no-parking sign, and then grabbed her hot-pink oversized purse before heading for the motorcycle shop.

She didn't know a single thing about motorcycles, but when she'd interviewed for the job, Kade had told her that didn't matter. What he needed was someone to answer the phones and take appointments. She would have other light duties like filing papers, making sure tags got on the keys when clients dropped them off, and keeping the reception area stocked with coffee and sodas.

She could do all of that. At least, she hoped she could. She really needed this job.

When Addie had first arrived in town, she'd gotten a small studio apartment, bought a reliable used car, and signed up for classes at the university. She'd emptied her checking account before she'd left home, and it had been a sizable chunk of money, but it wouldn't last forever.

It was time for Addie to join the workforce.

Taking a deep breath, she headed for the door leading to the reception area. The garage bays were open, and several men were working in them, but no one noticed her.

As soon as she stepped inside, she startled because she was greeted with a squeal of excitement. After her initial shock, she realized Eden had jumped up from a chair. Her friend rushed forward to give her a hug.

"I'm so glad you're here." Eden released her, grinning. "I figured maybe you wouldn't have had a chance to eat breakfast, so I had Bear make you pancakes." She pointed toward a covered dish sitting on the counter.

Addie was overwhelmed. It was true that all she'd had this morning so far was coffee. She'd been too nervous to eat anything, and there was no way she would be able to swallow pancakes. They would sit like a brick in her stomach. "Thank you. That's so nice. You didn't have to do that."

Eden shrugged. "I wanted you to feel welcomed on your first day." Eden was bubbly and way too excited. Her red curls were in low pigtails behind her ears. She often wore them that way to class.

Her ginormous boyfriend, Gabriel, was right behind her. The man was always with her. The only place he seemed to let Eden go without him was into her classes at the university, though he waited outside.

At first, Addie had thought it was incredibly strange how Gabriel always hovered as though he were a jealous boyfriend. Addie had been extremely skeptical. In fact, she'd been leery about meeting with Eden for a study date the first time they'd made a plan.

Eden had told Addie right away that Gabriel would most likely come with her because he was overprotective. Super weird in Addie's opinion, but Eden was the only person in her algebra class who was even close to Addie's age of twenty-two. The rest of the class consisted mainly of eighteen-year-old freshmen.

After their first study session at the library, they'd met for coffee after class one day. Just as Eden had assumed, Gabriel had come with her for both events. The man had not said much, nor had he sat with them. He hadn't seemed to mind a bit that his girlfriend had friends or met with them. It became instantly clear that Gabriel literally followed her like a bodyguard. He always sat near the exit and watched everyone who came and went.

Addie hadn't asked a lot of questions. Clearly, Gabriel adored Eden and vice-versa. They'd even gotten engaged. Eden now wore a gorgeous diamond, which she had a tendency to spin around absently on her finger.

The thought of anyone getting married made Addie cringe inwardly, but she wouldn't tell Eden that.

The truth was that Eden was Addie's only friend in town. Until they'd met in class, Addie hadn't made friends with anyone. She'd still been constantly looking over her shoulder, worried Joseph would somehow find her.

He could if he wanted to. It wouldn't take long for a private investigator to locate her. Though she'd left town with all the cash from her account and hadn't opened a new bank account yet, she had used her social security number to apply for jobs and enter school.

Addie wasn't particularly worried about Joseph. She couldn't imagine why the man would care that she'd left him at the altar. They'd hardly known each other. Except for the fact that she might have embarrassed him, he'd surely walked away that day without losing a moment's sleep.

Her mother, on the other hand, was probably livid. But it had been three months now. No one had knocked on Addie's door. None of them would be able to reach her by phone because she'd disabled it and tossed it in a trash can as soon as she'd stepped into the airport. When she'd arrived in town, she'd gotten a new phone and a new number.

Nevertheless, she wasn't in deep hiding. She knew it wouldn't take much effort for someone to figure out her address and her new number. They had not, so she was starting to breathe easier. Maybe no one cared she'd left town...?

That was both depressing and a relief.

Gabriel set a hand on Eden's shoulder and reached around her to hold out a hand. "Welcome to Shadowridge Guardians, Addie."

Addie shook his hand. "Thank you." She looked around. Gabriel wasn't her boss. Kade was. At least, that's what she thought.

"Kade will be here in a moment," Gabriel continued. "He got called into the shop to help with a motor."

Addie nodded. She felt awkward. She *always* felt awkward in new situations. That had been true her entire life. Or maybe it was simply that she'd rarely been in any situations where she'd felt like she belonged.

Even from a young age, Addie had felt like her mother's puppet. She'd been an agreeable child and had done as she was told most of the time, but she'd had the sense she'd been switched at birth.

Her parents were wealthy, and now there was just her mother. Caroline had come from what Addie had learned was considered "old money." Her father had been a banker, so he'd earned money in his own right, but it had been her mother whose lifestyle they'd all fallen in line with.

Nannies, tutors, private music lessons, sports teams—Addie hadn't had any interest in any of it. She'd gone to an elite private school and had been a good girl who'd gotten an English degree because "it was a respectable degree for a debutante."

Vomit.

If her father had still been alive, she was pretty sure he would have helped Addie talk her mother into letting her get a degree in something that included math, but he'd passed and left her to fend for herself.

Addie had been a zombie for the past five years since her father's sudden heart attack. She'd been much closer to him than her mother. She'd felt a kinship with him. Since then, she'd let her mother railroad her into all kinds of things, including her degree and the selection of a husband.

The pressure had been building inside Addie for a long time. The need to get out from under her mother's thumb had grown and grown until she'd finally snapped. She felt bad about coming to her senses one minute before her wedding, but that had been the moment she'd jolted into her body and taken control of her life.

It could have been worse. She could have gone through with the farce of a wedding and spent the next several years slowly dying while pretending to care about a man she had no feelings for. What if they'd had kids? She shuddered.

"Do you want to eat pancakes while you wait?" Eden asked.

"Uhh..."

Gabriel chuckled. "How about we let Addie get settled in? I doubt she wants to sit down and eat right this second."

"Right." Eden nodded. "Well, you can stick them in the microwave and reheat them when you're ready."

Gabriel winked at Addie from behind Eden. He understood she might not want them, but he was humoring his fiancée.

The door leading to the shop opened, and Kade stepped in, wiping his hands on a towel. "I'm so sorry I wasn't here to meet you, Addie. I think I got everything situated in the shop, so I can show you around now."

Gabriel pulled Eden back toward yet another door behind the reception desk. "Let's let Addie get settled in. You can come check on her at lunch."

"Okay, D— I mean, okay. Good idea." Eden beamed at Addie. "Have a great first day."

"Thank you." Even though Addie didn't know a single thing about motorcycle clubs or motorcycles in general, she was grateful for this job. She knew good and well she'd only been hired because of Eden.

As soon as Eden and Gabriel were gone, she turned her attention to Kade.

He waved her farther into the room from where she was still standing just inside the entrance. "Come on around the receptionist's desk. There's a place you can safely stow your purse." He glanced at the covered plate on the counter and chuckled. "Let me guess. Eden had Bear make you pancakes."

"Uh, yes. Who's Bear?"

"Another club member. You'll meet him eventually. He often hangs around the clubhouse and wanders into the shop. He's the club's secretary. You'll like him. He's a big guy. Don't let his size freak you out when you meet him. I'm pretty sure inside him lives a giant teddy bear, which is fitting. All the girls adore him. Mostly because he makes them pancakes in the morning."

"Girls?"

He winced. "Sorry. Women."

She nodded. For a moment, she'd thought maybe there were children living here. Maybe there were?

"Ready for a tour?"

"Yes." She stowed her purse in the box he indicated under the counter and glanced at the plate of food.

"Don't worry about the pancakes. No one's feelings will be hurt if you don't feel like eating them, or maybe you don't even like pancakes." He chuckled. "Eden can be pushy."

Addie hated to risk hurting anyone's feelings, so she would try to eat them, but not yet. Right now, she was too nervous about learning her way around this job.

CHAPTER
THREE

When Bear stepped into the reception area later that morning, he didn't see anyone at first. He was behind the desk. He squinted into the sunlight streaming in from the front windows as a slight movement caught his eye.

Someone was over in the corner. She must have been squatting down, reaching for something in the cabinet under the beverage center. As she rose with her back to him, he drew in a breath.

Was this Addie? She was incredibly petite with long, silky black hair. But what stood out was the halo that seemed to hover above her. It was simply a trick of the sunlight, but it made her look like an angel.

He watched as she stocked the counter with coffee pods, creamers, and sugar. He hadn't seen her face yet, but he could tell she was dainty. Her fingers were tiny. So was her waist and even her hips. Her hair was a glossy curtain that swayed back and forth as she moved.

Bear held his breath as he waited for her to turn around, which was probably a bad idea because when she finally spun, she yelped and nearly jumped out of her skin. He'd scared her to death.

"Shit. I'm sorry." He took a step forward, even more mesmerized now that he could see her face. Damn, she was pretty. Rosy cheeks, a button nose, full pink lips, and green eyes a man could get lost in.

"I didn't hear you," she murmured, breathing heavily.

He stopped himself from advancing farther as he realized he was scaring her. She had no idea who he was, and he was far more than twice her size. "I'm so sorry," he repeated. "I didn't mean to scare you, Little one."

Was she Little? He had no idea.

Her gaze darted from him to the counter, and when he followed it, he noticed the covered plate of pancakes. When he looked back at her, she winced. "Are you Bear?"

He grinned. "I am. I guess you've heard about me. I assume you're Adelaine?"

"Addie," she whispered. "I'm so sorry about the pancakes. I, uh, my nerves, and…"

Ah, the Little angel was worried about hurting his feelings. "No problem, Angel. Don't you worry. Eden was so excited about you being here this morning that she insisted I fix you a plate. Obviously, she didn't take into consideration the fact that you might have already eaten, or perhaps you don't like pancakes, or that nervous jitters on your first day would make it hard for you to eat."

She slowly gifted him with the most beautiful smile as her shoulders relaxed. "I do like pancakes," she murmured.

"Then I'll whisk these away and make you some another day. How does that sound?"

The smile grew. "Thank you."

As he picked up the plate, she lurched forward. "But…"

"What, Little one?"

She chewed on the corner of her lower lip for a moment,

contemplating something before answering. "I should eat them so I don't hurt Eden's feelings."

Bear tipped his head back and laughed harder than he had in a long time. After wiping his eyes, he found her staring at him wide-eyed, mouth open.

"My apologies again, Addie." She was so thoughtful. He set the plate back down, lifted the lid, and cut off a bite of pancake. After dipping it into the syrup, he held a hand under it and reached toward her. "If you eat one bite, you can truthfully tell Eden they were delicious."

Her adorable smile came back, and she giggled. "We don't know that yet. I'll be able to truthfully tell her I *tried* them. What if they're yucky?"

He laughed again. Damn, she was something. His heart was beating faster than it had in a long time. He couldn't remember when a woman had last caught his attention. A very long time, that was for sure. "You've got me there. It's worth a try, though, right?"

She closed the distance and opened her pretty mouth.

Bear's cock jumped to full attention as he fed this precious Little girl a bite of pancake. The sweet thing even closed her eyes as she thoughtfully chewed and swallowed.

He held his breath the entire time, knowing without a doubt this Little angel had stolen his heart. "Well?"

She smiled again. "I bet they were better a few hours ago, but they're delicious." She tapped her lips. "To be sure, I should probably try another bite."

Bear's heart stopped as he cut her another bite, making sure to include chocolate chips. He dipped the bite in the syrup and held it out.

Addie leaned in closer, accepted the bite, and grinned. "Yep. Delicious. Thank you."

He set the fork on the plate and dropped the lid over it before meeting her gaze again. "I'm glad you like them. I assume if you won't lie to Eden, you won't lie to me either."

She shook her head, all that gorgeous hair flying around her shoulders. "I'm not a good liar. I'm really good at omitting the truth, though, when it's necessary. This is one of those situations where I'm pretty sure Eden is going to bound out here in a bit and flat-out ask me how the pancakes were."

Yep. Adorable. And what the hell was Bear thinking? He had no business standing here flirting with this woman, even if she was Little. He had no idea if that was true or not, but as strong as his Daddy instincts were, he made a much better Uncle to the other Littles in the club than an actual Daddy to anyone.

Sobering at this thought, he decided he really should get away from this woman before he lost his head. After picking up the plate, he gave her a slight bow. "It was nice meeting you, Addie. I hope you enjoy working here."

"Thank you." She gave him another award-winning smile as he backed out of the room.

Jesus. What had gotten into him? For a few minutes, he'd taken leave of his senses and had found himself wishing the raven-haired pixie could be his.

Bear hurried back to the kitchen, quickly disposed of the cold pancakes, and put the dishes in the dishwasher. When he spun around, he discovered the kitchen was spotless, so he needed to find something else to do to occupy his mind.

Hiding seemed like a good plan. He could go to his apartment, type up the notes from the latest club meeting, and... And then what? He really needed to get a hobby. He'd been spending too much time in the clubhouse, helping his brothers with their Littles. He'd loved every moment of it, but it must have gone to his head, causing him to suddenly lust after the first single Little girl he'd seen in a long time.

That had to have been what had happened. It had been a long time since he'd dated anyone. He'd been watching his brothers moon over their Littles, and he'd been basically babysitting them with far too much frequency. He should cut that out. Make himself scarce and too busy.

After entering his apartment, he ran a hand through his thick hair and began to pace. He would be lying to himself if he didn't admit the last several months had been far more entertaining now that several of his brothers had found their Littles. Laughter and shenanigans filled the clubhouse.

Bear had loved every minute of it.

He dropped down on the couch, propped his elbows on his knees, and leaned his forehead against his palms. Squeezing his eyes shut, he tried to block the memories that flooded in unbidden.

"I can't do this anymore, Eddie. I've tried—Lord knows I've tried— but the truth is, there's something seriously wrong with you."

"Valerie…" He had no idea how to respond to her. She'd dropped this huge bomb in his lap, and he was speechless.

"You need to see a therapist," she continued as she stuffed more of her things into a giant suitcase. "It's not normal for a grown man to want to treat his girlfriend like she's a Little girl."

Bile rose in his throat. They'd been together for over a year. He'd thought she was the perfect Little for him, and now, suddenly…

If he were honest with himself, there had been signs that Valerie had been unhappy. She'd started spending more and more time out of the house, hanging with her friends. Even when she'd been at home, she'd given him every excuse she could come up with not to submit to him.

She was too tired. She had too much work to do. She wasn't in the mood for coloring. The list was long.

"How long have you felt this way?" he asked in the calmest voice he could manage. Meanwhile, he stood rooted to his spot in the middle of their bedroom, watching helplessly while the woman he'd intended to spend his life with packed her belongings.

She groaned and rolled her eyes. "Since you first mentioned the idea, Eddie."

His breath hitched. "Then why the hell did you go along with it? Why did you move in with me? Why did you waste a year of our lives pretending to enjoy the same kink as me if you didn't care for it?"

She turned toward him, put her hands on her hips, and shot him a glare. "Are you serious?"

He lifted both brows, confused. "Yes, Valerie. I'm serious. Answer the question."

She rolled her eyes. "Eddie, you're so dense sometimes." She turned back around and closed her suitcase. "Money, Eddie. It was always about the money."

He stopped breathing. The room was spinning. His heart felt like it would leap out of his chest. "You dated me because I have money?"

She jerked her suitcase off the bed and let it hit the floor with a thud. "Yes, big guy. I thought you were the entire package. Tall, dark, and handsome, in addition to funny, smart, and kind. But more importantly, you're rich."

More importantly? That was harsh and hit him so hard he nearly stumbled backward.

She pulled her suitcase past him and turned around at the door. "Word of advice. Next time you meet a woman you like, don't tell her you have any money. That's the only way you'll know if she authentically cares about you. You're a nice guy, Eddie. I wish I could be the woman you want, but I just can't do it. Lord knows, I tried. It would've been nice spending my life without having to worry about how to pay the rent. But in the end, it's not worth it. I'm not Little. I'm a grown woman. Good luck, Eddie."

He stared at the open doorway, listening to her lug that suitcase down the stairs. He flinched when the front door shut but otherwise didn't move an inch for a long time.

The house was too quiet without her. Though, again, if he was honest with himself, the house had been quiet most of the time for months because that's how long it had been since she'd last spent much time here. It had been even longer since she'd laughed with him or looked at him with those doe eyes.

He was a fool. He'd been so into her that he'd lied to himself for a very long time. In his mind, he'd accepted all her excuses and pretended she would eventually come around.

It hadn't happened, and now, she was gone.

He wouldn't be heeding her advice, though. He wouldn't need to lie to his next girlfriend and pretend he didn't have a sizable inheritance.

Because there wouldn't be a next time.

CHAPTER
FOUR

"**B**ear?"

The hair on the back of Bear's neck stood on end at the sound of his name being shouted from one of the Littles. He was pretty sure it was Eden, and as he turned around from where he'd been stirring a pot of chili at the stove, sure enough, Eden burst into the room.

Her eyes were wide with...fear?

"What is it, Little one?" He set the spoon down and hurried toward her.

She was breathing heavily, as if she'd run hard to get to him. She pointed over her shoulder. "Addie is stuck in the bathroom. In the shop. I went to check on her, and I couldn't find her, and then I heard her calling out from inside the bathroom."

Eden grabbed his hand and tugged him in that direction, but she didn't need to. He was already running. Damn, that knob. It had been acting with a mind of its own for weeks. Now, he was furious with himself for not fixing it.

He jogged through the clubhouse and into the front office of the motorcycle shop, where he skidded to a stop outside the bathroom at the back of the reception area. "Addie? It's Bear. You okay?" He grabbed the handle and jiggled it. All it did was spin. *Shit.*

"Yeah. Just...embarrassed."

"No reason to be embarrassed. I'm sorry you're stuck. I should've fixed this knob a while ago. What's it doing on your side?"

"It just spins." Same as his side then.

"Okay. Hang tight for me. I'm going to grab some tools and take the knob off. If that doesn't work, I'll pop off the door."

"Thank you," she said softly. "I'm sorry."

He drew in a breath. "Not your fault, Little one. I promise."

The door leading to the shop opened, and Kade stepped in. "What's wrong?" he asked as he glanced back and forth between Bear and Eden.

Eden threw her hands up in the air and practically wailed. "The door knob finally decided it was done working altogether, and Addie is stuck in the bathroom."

Bear felt pretty bad about the situation, especially because he should have fixed it before now, but it was hard not to chuckle at Eden's dramatics. This wasn't exactly a life-or-death situation. After all, if a person had to be trapped somewhere, they'd want the space to have water and a toilet.

But these were Little girls he was dealing with. When Littles got fully into their space, everything was a drama. Eden was clearly there now.

Kade turned toward the shop. "I'll grab the toolbox."

Gabriel dashed into the room from the rear entrance. "What happened? I got a text from Eden that there was an emergency."

Bear shot Eden a narrow-eyed, stern look. "Eden..."

Eden's cheeks pinkened, and she clasped her hands behind her back and rocked on her feet. "What? It *is* an emergency." She turned toward her Daddy. "Addie is *stuck* in there." More drama.

Why am I about to laugh?

It wasn't funny that Addie was trapped in the bathroom, but it was humorous that Eden thought it was an international event. But even more poignant was how damn cute she was, with her eyes widening with the intensity of her emotions. Why did these Littles have to tug at his heartstrings so hard?

Gabriel set his hands on her shoulders from behind and pulled her back. "Let me guess. You *ran* through the clubhouse to get Bear to come help."

"She sure did," Bear agreed, not the least bit bothered by throwing her under the bus.

"Tattletale," she blurted at the same time she stuck her tongue out.

If Addie hadn't known Eden was Little before now, she certainly was getting an education. Bear just hoped it didn't cause her to run from the club and never come back.

And why would I care if she didn't return? He'd spent the day giving himself a pep talk that involved not letting himself think about the Little angel working so very close all day while frequently reminding himself he needed to keep his distance. And now this.

Kade returned with a toolbox.

Bear grabbed the Phillips screwdriver and quickly removed the knob, which disengaged the mechanism. "Addie, can you pull the knob on your side out of the hole?"

She wiggled it free, and he bent to examine the hole. "Good job." He reached his middle finger through the small hole to pull the lever back and disengage the door.

When it popped free, it swung open in his direction, and he removed his fingers and opened it farther.

Addie stood inside, rubbing her hands together. Her cheeks were dark pink. "Thank you," she muttered.

"No problem. I'm sorry this happened. I bet you were scared."

"Only because it took a while before Eden came into the room and heard me calling out."

Eden rushed into the bathroom and pulled Addie in for a hug. "I'm so sorry."

Addie took a deep breath and stepped out. "I'm fine now."

Gabriel cleared his throat. "My apologies, too, Addie. If you'll excuse us for a bit..." He took Eden's shoulders firmly in his hands.

Eden sighed heavily and rolled her eyes.

Bear was a little shocked by her blatant display of age play in front of Addie. As far as he knew, Eden didn't let her Little out in public, including at the university.

"I'll be back later," she groaned as Gabriel turned her around and guided her toward the rear entrance that led to the clubhouse.

Addie stared at the door for a long time as it closed. Finally, she turned back to face Bear.

Kade cleared his throat. "Yeah, I'm gonna let you handle this, man. I'll be in the shop." He turned and jogged back through the adjoining door as though the room were on fire.

Asshole. Bear never took his gaze off Addie, though.

Addie cocked her head. "Is he, uh..." She licked her pretty lips. "Gabriel. I mean, is he going to...spank her?"

Bear let one corner of his mouth tip up. At least he wasn't going to have to explain things quite as thoroughly as he'd feared. He would get back at both Kade and Gabriel for abandoning him here to talk to Addie. Someone else should be doing this. *Anyone* else.

"Definitely." No sense beating around the bush.

"Why...exactly?" Her eyes were wide with curiosity as opposed to disgust.

"The simple answer? Because she likes it."

Addie licked her lips again and... *My God.* She rubbed her palms together and shifted her weight around nervously. Her pink cheeks turned pinker. She was intrigued. "You keep calling me Little."

"I do." If she was going to explain their entire way of life to him without him needing to contribute, he would let her.

Addie once again glanced at the door where Eden and Gabriel had disappeared. "I've read about this. I didn't know it was a real thing."

Thank fuck. "It's very real for a lot of people. I know Eden doesn't ordinarily let her Little out in front of people not inside her bubble, but I suspect having you here at the MC has caused her to have trouble straddling the line," he explained.

"Because she's Little when she's here. When she's home."

"Yes."

She held his gaze again. "And no one minds?"

"Most of the members of this MC are involved in the age-play community to some extent. Most of the men are Daddies. Most of the girlfriends and wives are Littles."

She took a step back and then another until her back was against the wall. "Are *you* a Daddy?"

"Yes."

"Why would you assume I'm Little?"

He gave her a slow smile. "I have excellent Little radar."

She swallowed hard. "But that's not fair."

He furrowed his brow, confused. "What's not fair, Little one?"

She shivered when he used that endearment. "I've never even thought about it before. How could you know something about me before me?"

Fuck, but she was precious. She was in no way denying the accuracy of his observation. Instead, she was ticked off that he'd realized it before her. Adorable. He shrugged. "Angel, it just happens sometimes. Like you said, you didn't realize age play was a real thing outside of books. Therefore, you have never considered it as more than just a titillating fantasy. That doesn't mean you don't have a Little inside you who'd love to come out and play."

He shouldn't be nudging her like this. He should be fixing the door and leaving her alone. He didn't want to give her the wrong idea. Even though he'd suspected she had a Little inside her and could benefit from a Daddy's firm hand, that didn't mean he was offering himself. He wasn't. He couldn't.

"Do you have a Little girl of your own?"

Shit. He inhaled slowly. "No, Little one, I don't. I did once. It didn't work out." *Tell her. Tell her you're not interested in taking that kind of risk again. Tell her it was too painful.*

Bear did neither. Instead, he pointed toward the door. "I'm going to run to the hardware store and get a new knob. If you need to use the potty again this afternoon, there are several inside the clubhouse. Someone can show you where."

She stared at him, breathing heavily. "Will you be back soon?"

Fuck. Her voice was filled with hope. He couldn't let her hold on to that hope. "I'll wait until this evening to fix the door so I don't get in your way."

"Oh, okay. Sure. Right." She lowered her gaze and scurried behind the receptionist's desk to pick up a pile of papers and straighten them. "Thanks for helping me."

"You're welcome." *Angel.* This time, he held back the endearment. "Have a great rest of your day." It took every ounce of his willpower to turn and walk out of the room. As soon as he shut the door behind him, he found Kade in the shop and called out, "I'm heading to the hardware store. I'll fix that knob this evening."

"Thanks, man. I should've fixed it weeks ago, but we've been swamped here lately."

"No problem." Bear hurried out of the shop, aiming for his bike. He needed to put some distance between him and Addie. He needed to stay away until after she got off work.

After mounting his bike, he shot off a text to Gabriel.

"Heading to the hardware store. Chili is simmering on the stove. Keep an eye on it." He stuffed his phone in his pocket and started the engine. The hum between his thighs calmed him somewhat, but the truth was nothing was going to calm the Pandora's box that got split wide open today the moment he'd seen that sweet Little angel.

Fuck.

CHAPTER
FIVE

"Addie?"

The small voice coming from behind Addie belonged to Eden, and she turned around to face her friend.

"Hi." Eden looked nervous and chagrined. "I owe you an apology."

"For what?"

"For a lot of things. Bear told me he spoke with you about...everything." Eden glanced over her shoulder.

Addie nodded as she noticed Gabriel standing on the other side of the open door, arms crossed, brows lifted. She was seeing him in a new light today.

She'd never been able to put her finger on what it was about him all the times she'd previously seen him. It wasn't that he was some sort of bodyguard or crazy jealous boyfriend.

Addie had spent a lot of time this afternoon thinking about every encounter with Gabriel. He was a Daddy. It all made sense now. He hovered because that was their dynamic. He hovered because he adored Eden and wanted her to be safe and protected. He hovered because he liked being with her.

It was so damn sweet that Addie found herself feeling jealous. She'd certainly never had a relationship that had come anywhere close to the one Eden and Gabriel had. Her fiancé certainly hadn't hovered. Ha. The man had barely glanced at her at any point in their "relationship." Thank God she hadn't married him.

Eden continued. "It was wrong of me to point out there was a job opening here in the motorcycle shop without telling you anything about the MC. I specifically should've told you I was Little because there was no way you could have spent any amount of time here without figuring it out. Plus, I realized today that I'm not very good at being in my adult headspace when I'm here."

"It's okay. I understand. I would've had trouble telling anyone if I were in your shoes, too."

"Anyway, I'm sorry. I also shouldn't have misbehaved intentionally in front of you. I'm sure it made you uncomfortable knowing I was getting my bottom spanked. It wasn't very sensitive of me."

Addie offered her a smile. "It's all good, Eden. I was a bit surprised for a moment, but I figured it out. I've read books."

"Have you?" Eden drew in a breath, her shoulders relaxing in relief.

Addie shrugged. "Sure. I mean, I didn't know it was a thing in real life, but I'm not judgmental." *How could I be?* If anyone knew the mistakes she'd made... They'd be shocked far more than she'd been today.

"You've read...a *lot* of books about Daddies and Littles?"

"I guess," she murmured, not sure she wanted to admit such a thing. The truth was she'd spent years living in a world where everyone had been fake, and she'd been expected to maintain a fake marriage for the rest of her life so her family would look good.

Books about age play had been her escape. Even though she'd thought the entire concept was nothing more than a fantasy, she'd always enjoyed pretending there were people in the world who lived authentically, even if their lifestyle choices went against the norm.

Age play definitely went against the norm—except, apparently, inside this MC. According to Bear, most of the members were Daddies and Littles. She hadn't fully wrapped her mind around that.

Ironically, Addie had spent the last several months feeling like she needed to find and maintain a backbone. She needed to stop letting people order her around and tell her what to do. She needed to make her own decisions in life.

The reason she was in this town was to start fresh and to make her own choices. She was even taking classes so she could work toward a degree she enjoyed instead of the one she'd let herself get sucked into. She was paying for everything with money she'd earned instead of an allowance given to her by her mother.

When she'd first been left alone to think about the bathroom incident this afternoon, she'd shuddered at the thought of women turning their choices over to men and letting them make decisions for them. That's exactly what she'd run from.

But after a while, she'd begun to see it through a different lens. Gabriel adored Eden. His world revolved around her. He Daddied her because she wanted him to. What would it feel like to have someone care about Addie the way Gabriel cared about Eden? She couldn't begin to imagine.

Maybe her father had doted on her that way when she'd been a child, but since his death, not a single person had looked her in the eye with love and affection. Certainly not her mother or her fiancé.

The first person to hold her gaze and give her every ounce of his attention in years had been Bear, and he obviously had only been interested in helping her get out of the bathroom. He'd made that clear when he'd told her he would wait for her to be gone before he came to fix the doorknob.

"Well, I just wanted to apologize, and also, now that you

know, anytime you want to come here and study, you can do that, or if you want to come over and just hang out, that would be fun, too."

"Thank you. I might take you up on that." Addie twisted around when the door to the shop opened. It happened from time to time throughout the day, and she was continually looking to see who was coming in.

It was Kade again this time. He glanced at his watch. "What are you still doing here, Addie? It's almost six. You get off at five."

She absently tidied up the desk a bit. The job was cushy. Most of the day, she'd spent making sure the coffee pods were stocked, answering the phone, and organizing the files for each client who had a bike in the shop. "Well, I lost quite a bit of time when I was stuck in the bathroom, and—"

Kade frowned. "That was not your fault. That was *my* fault. And I'm so very sorry about that. I was afraid you would run out the front door and not come back."

She shook her head. "No, sir. It was no big deal. Weird things happen sometimes."

Kade glanced toward the door where the old knob still sat against the wall. "Bear didn't come back and fix it yet? He left a long time ago to get a new knob."

"Yeah. He, uh, he said he would do it later tonight when I'm not here."

Kade frowned again. "Why on Earth would he do that?"

Addie was pretty sure the question was rhetorical, and she certainly wasn't going to share her theory that he was avoiding her, so she said nothing.

Eden came up beside her. "He got back a long time ago. I saw him in the kitchen and later in his office."

Addie drew in a deep breath. "Well, he didn't want to bother me," she added.

"Bother you?" Eden's brows furrowed. "That's silly."

Addie shrugged. "I guess I should go. I have some homework to do tonight."

Kade nodded. "What time did you say your class is tomorrow?"

"It's at eleven. Is that okay? I know it's inconvenient for me to leave for two hours. My other class is at night."

"It's not a problem at all, Addie," Kade said. "Don't you worry."

"I'll come in at eight on Mondays, Wednesdays, and Fridays to make up for the extra hour."

Kade rubbed his chin. "Okay, as long as it doesn't become too much for you. The shop will survive without you for two hours. Either I or one of the other guys will keep an eye on things. Customers can leave messages. You can call them back in the afternoon. And, Addie, I'm really glad you're here. It's so helpful having someone present in the office. I know there are lulls in the day. Feel free to do your homework or study, okay? Your education comes first. This is just a job. If you need time off for a test or something, let me know."

"Thank you, sir."

He shook his head, grinning. "Call me Kade, Addie. I expect Remi to call me Sir. Sometimes, the other Littles who hang around or live here call me Sir, but unless you hook up with one of my brothers, I'm just Kade to you."

She swallowed hard. These Daddy figures were so intense.

"Have you met Remi yet?" Eden asked.

Addie shook her head. "No."

Kade palmed his forehead. "Right. Sorry. She's my Little girl. You'll meet her soon. Have a nice night." He turned around, muttering something about shenanigans.

Eden giggled. "Oh, definitely."

"What?" Addie asked, confused.

"Eden..." Gabriel chastised.

Addie had forgotten he was hovering behind them.

Eden rolled her eyes. "Daddy..."

He'd spoken in a deep voice, the one Addie was coming to recognize as his Daddy voice. She understood much better now. His tone was chastising, but it was laced with humor and adoration. He loved that Eden misbehaved, and she loved it, too. It was so fascinating.

"It's Addie's first day here," Gabriel said. "You've bombarded her with information that was more overwhelming than the new job. Let her settle in for a few days before you drag her into your naughty plots."

Addie bit her lip, fighting back the urge to laugh.

Yeah, this entire MC was a fascinating place. She almost couldn't wait to meet the other women and join in whatever shenanigans Kade spoke of.

CHAPTER
SIX

T wo weeks later…

"So, all the girls are going to be here tonight. Gabriel is making us dinner. Bear is going to make us popcorn and hot chocolate. He makes the *best* hot chocolate in the world." Eden groaned. "You're still going to stay and join us, right?"

Addie had her back to the desk as she faced her friend. This tended to happen a lot since she'd started working here. She'd gradually met all of the women who were girlfriends and Littles to several of the club members, and they had a tendency to pop through the door at her back and talk to her throughout the day.

Remi was behind Eden, grinning. "You *have* to stay. It's going to be so much fun."

Addie was smart. She knew by now that "fun" was a code-word for, *We intend to get into all kinds of trouble so that we end up getting spanked.*

It was the most bizarre world. Grown women who lived as

Littles to the most gorgeous, giant, overprotective men on earth. Before Addie had taken this job, she'd known very little about motorcycle clubs. She'd always pictured something more along the lines of crime and drugs and loose women hanging around hoping to get laid.

Addie couldn't speak for any other motorcycle club, but the Shadowridge Guardians were nothing like what her wild imagination had conjured up. Sure, these men were large and assuming. Most of them had a lot of tattoos. Most had beards. However much they might look ominous, they were the nicest, most genuine people she'd ever met.

In the past two weeks, nearly all of them had stopped in to introduce themselves at some point or another. Everyone had been polite, welcoming, and kind. Even though she didn't have a boyfriend in the club, they treated her like she was one of them. They inquired about her car, making sure it was running well. They fretted over her safety, ensuring she carried pepper spray from her car to her apartment when she went home. They offered help with her algebra class if she needed it. They were truly the best people.

The women had asked her to join them after work nearly every day. Did she want to stay for dinner? Watch a movie with them? Play games? Do homework? So far, she'd turned them down.

The truth was she felt like a bit of an outsider. She didn't have a boyfriend in the club, which made her feel strange. She was, however, intrigued. She'd spent a lot of time on the internet researching real people who lived as Littles.

It seemed most of these women had jobs where they had to "adult" during the day, but when they got back to the clubhouse, they shed that side of themselves. Most of them seemed to have entire wardrobes filled with clothes appropriate for much younger girls. She'd caught glimpses of them with stuffed animals clutched in their arms. She was pretty sure she'd even seen a pacifier or two.

As the days went by, she'd found herself feeling kind of jealous. She'd also found it impossible not to fantasize about the one man who stood out in her mind when she crawled into bed. She'd tried reading to keep from thinking about him, but her mind always strayed to Bear.

Since that first day, she'd only seen him in passing. It was obvious he was avoiding her, and she had no idea why. She'd gotten self-conscious about it. Had she said something wrong or done something to displease him?

Addie hadn't had the guts to ask Eden if she knew anything because she'd been afraid of the answer. If she joined the women tonight, would Bear make himself scarce and hide in his apartment?

She had learned that most club members had their own small apartments in the clubhouse. Some of them had houses in town, too. But some of them lived in the clubhouse full-time. She knew Bear lived here full-time, which made it all the more obvious he was avoiding her like she had a communicable disease.

The most mysterious component of this lifestyle was this seemingly endless desire to get spanked. All the women intentionally did naughty things in order to get their butts swatted.

So far, no one had gotten spanked in front of Addie, but she suspected if she were to join them tonight, she would witness an entire host of new experiences, spanking included.

And how did that make her feel? She wasn't sure. She wasn't sure how she felt about anything regarding age play yet. Could she let someone order her around? Reading about it was hot. Doing it? Yeah, that made her cringe. But spanking? That was an entirely different level of intensity. The thought of being taken over a man's knees and letting him swat her butt...

"Addie?"

She jerked out of her musing to find that Elizabeth had

joined Eden and Remi. The three of them were leaning through the door, waiting for her to respond.

Elizabeth, Talon's girlfriend, was a lawyer, Remi was an artist, and Eden was a student. There were three other girlfriends, and Addie thought she had them all straight. Ivy was a bank manager. Her boyfriend was the club's president, Steele. Carlee worked at the library. Her boyfriend was the club's treasurer, Atlas. And Harper was a cake decorator. Her boyfriend was their doctor, who went by Doc.

"Okay, sure. I'll stay."

The three of them jumped up and down. "Yay!"

Addie giggled. She so badly wanted to be a part of their fun. After all, she didn't have other friends in town yet. Eden had been the first person she'd developed a relationship with, and the other women she'd met at the MC were the only other friends she had, even if their relationships were a bit peripheral.

The sad thing was that she felt closer to all six of them than she had any other supposed friend in recent years. Hell, she was so pitiful that she hadn't even known the women who'd been her intended bridesmaids.

"I'm so excited," Eden exclaimed. "We're going to have so much fun."

The tinkling of the bell over the door to the reception area jingled, indicating someone had entered the shop, but Kade and two other employees were currently standing on the other side of the desk discussing a particular paint job, so it wasn't surprising that Kade greeted the newcomer.

"Good afternoon. What can we do for you?"

The voice that responded caused Addie's blood to run cold. For a moment, she stood there frozen, unable to move a single muscle. Surely, she was mistaken.

"I've got an old bike that belonged to my father. It's been in storage for many years. Decades really. I was wondering if someone could take a look at it and see if it's worth salvaging."

At some point in the middle of that speech, Addie had instinctively dropped down behind the counter. She sat on her butt, plastered against the back of the tall reception desk, and pulled her knees up to her chest.

This could not be happening.

When she glanced at the three women, she found them with wide eyes and sober faces. They nodded as they backed out of the doorway. Eden held up a finger before the door closed, indicating she was going to get help.

Addie's heart raced. Had Joseph found her? Was he here to torment her for leaving him at the altar? Or was it a coincidence?

It made no sense. She was three states away from her old life. What was her fiancé doing in this town, asking about an old bike? She found it super unlikely he owned a bike or that his father ever had either. It wasn't possible to picture Joseph Bulgari, Senior or Junior, on a motorcycle.

Kade was talking to him, but she couldn't focus on what they were saying. All she could do was pray no one saw her or called out her name.

Please, God... She started rocking back and forth as panic seeped in.

Suddenly, the door in front of her opened again. This time, Bear stepped inside. She was shocked, but she should have realized that's who Eden would go to for help. The man seemed to always be in the clubhouse. All the Littles adored him and went to him.

His brow was furrowed with concern as he glanced at her without lingering. He stepped up to the desk next to her and set his palm gently on the top of her head before letting it slide around to cup her cheek reassuringly.

"Hey, Kade," he began, "I forgot to tell you the receptionist, Debra, had to leave early today. I told her I'd keep an eye on things. Do you need me for anything?"

Addie held her breath. Bless him.

Kade didn't miss a beat. "Nope. It's all good. I was just about to close up for the day anyway. This man has a bike he'd like us to look at. I told him he could leave it, and we'd check it out and see if it's salvageable."

Bear nodded. "Cool. You from around here? I haven't seen you before."

"Nope. I flew out here to pick up the bike. It was in storage. I figured I wouldn't bother having it transported back home if it isn't worth anything. I'll hang around town and wait to see what you think. When do you think you can look at it?"

"We'll get to it first thing tomorrow, Mr. Bulgari. Not a problem," Kade said.

"Please, Joe is fine."

Addie held her breath. *Joe?* Since when did anyone call him Joe? He was far too pretentious to use a nickname.

"Sounds good then, Joe," Kade continued. "You added your number to the paperwork, right?"

"Sure did."

"I'll be in touch sometime tomorrow then."

"Thank you. Appreciate it."

The bell above the door rang again, and the room went dead silent. For a moment, no one moved, not even Bear. He remained right where he was, his hand on Addie's cheek, soothing her as best he could.

She figured he was watching and waiting for Joseph to completely disappear. Finally, Kade was the first to speak. "What the fuck just happened?" His tone wasn't angry, just curious.

Bear dropped down to squat in front of Addie, taking her face in both hands. "Deep breaths. You're okay. Who was that, Little one?"

CHAPTER
SEVEN

Heart racing, Bear stared into his Little's wide green eyes. He'd never seen her so pale before. She was shaking violently and looked like she might vomit. "Can you tell me who that was, Little one?"

Tears started to run down her cheeks. "I'm so sorry. I didn't think he would look for me."

"It's okay. You're safe here. I promise." It was hard for Bear to keep his cool. He wanted to take off after that man and strangle him for whatever he'd done to put this fear in his Little girl's eyes.

And fuck. She was *definitely* his Little girl. He'd done everything in his power to ignore the pull toward her and deny he cared about her for the past two weeks, but it had been a losing battle.

The moment Eden, Elizabeth, and Remi had run to him, looking scared out of their minds, he'd been a goner for Addie. The last tiny sliver of denial he'd been holding on to dissolved before he'd even gotten the story out of Eden.

Bear had already been on his feet, jogging toward the shop as Eden told him about the man who'd come in and scared

Addie out of her mind enough that she was now huddled behind the desk.

It had taken every ounce of his self-control to calmly step into the reception area. He'd wanted to throw punches the moment he'd seen Addie curled in a tiny ball, hiding. Fury had consumed him, but he'd somehow managed to keep his shit together while sending Kade a message that something was not okay here.

He'd known if he referred to the receptionist as Debra, Kade would catch on and play along. So had the other men from the shop. No one even flinched. None of them were strangers to trouble. Lord knew they'd encountered enough crazy lately to last a lifetime.

There was no sense pretending Addie wasn't his Little girl in every sense of the word, so he scooped her off the floor, cradled her against his chest, and turned to head back into the clubhouse.

Someone grabbed his arm, and he turned to find Kade tucking a stuffed bear in next to Addie.

Grateful, Bear palmed Addie's head so her face was buried against him and headed straight for his apartment.

Whatever had spooked Addie wasn't something she would want to share with the entire club right now. It would be easier to get her to talk if they were alone.

As soon as he entered his apartment, he kicked the door shut and reached back to lock it. He aimed straight for the recliner and sat, holding Addie in his arms.

For several minutes, he just held her and rocked her, rubbing her back, her hair, her arm. His heart hurt as she sat so stiff, sniffling and telling him she was sorry over and over.

He kissed the top of her head and repeatedly told her it was okay and she was safe here. That was all he could do until she told him more. He didn't want to rush her and risk spooking her.

When her body finally started to relax, he leaned her back a few inches. "Look at Daddy, Angel."

Her breath hitched as she met his gaze, blinking.

"That's my good girl." He pulled the bear from where it was tucked under his arm and settled it under hers instead. "Maybe this little fellow will soothe you."

She glanced at the bear and back at him. "He's cute."

Bear picked up her hand and kissed her fingers. They were so tiny and soft. Her polish was a pretty shade of pink. She'd been wearing the same shade when he'd met her, so he figured it must be one of her favorite colors. "Is pink your favorite color, Little one?"

She nodded slowly. "But I don't own anything pink. Just the polish," she whispered.

"Why not?" It was such an odd response.

"Because grown women don't wear pink," she told him as if this were common knowledge.

He forced himself to remain calm. What he wanted to do was demand answers and then go after the fool who'd dared hurt his Little girl. But this method was going to work much better. "Who says?"

She shrugged. "My mother," she mumbled.

"Ah, well, that seems silly. I think all people should embrace whatever color they want. What about grown men? Are they allowed to wear pink?"

She giggled and shook her head. The sound warmed his heart.

"I'm ordering three pink shirts first thing tomorrow," he declared, smiling at her.

"For me?"

"Hell, no. For me."

She giggled again.

"Maybe I'll let you wear one."

"It would reach my knees."

"It could be a sleep shirt."

She stared at him for a moment. Perhaps she was starting to realize they'd moved into new territory. Did she know it was permanent?

He didn't give a fuck who that man out front had been or what demons she was fighting. He would take care of it and take care of her at the same time.

She licked those sexy pink lips. "Only if you wear it first."

Those words would have brought him to his knees if he'd been standing. His heart couldn't take it. "I'll wear a pink shirt every day from now on if you'll wear it to bed at night."

Her cheeks turned rosy, and her lips parted to speak again. "But you don't even like me."

Fuck. "That's not true, Angel. I adore you. I knew you were mine the first time I set eyes on you. You were standing at the counter next to the window, organizing the coffee and water. There was a halo around you from the sunshine, and your silky black hair was swaying down your back like an angel's hair."

Her eyes went wide. "But..."

He kissed her fingers again. "I'm an old fool."

"You haven't spoken to me since that first day."

"Like I said, I'm a fool."

"Why?"

He drew in a deep breath. He'd rather talk about her problems than hash out why he was such a fool, but this was what she needed first. "I had a Little girl once a long time ago. She hurt me, and I swore I would never let someone get close enough to me to hurt me again."

Addie searched his eyes. "She didn't deserve you."

He smiled. "No. She didn't. The truth is she wasn't Little. She was faking it. But I cared about her, and I was too enamored to notice that fact even though it was right in front of my face."

"How do you know I'm Little?"

"I'm wiser now."

"But *I* don't even know if I'm Little."

"You will, Angel. You just haven't had a chance to explore your Little side yet. I bet you've been thinking about it, though."

She nodded. "All the time. I have so many questions."

"That's okay. You'll ask all of them whenever you're ready. Either I or someone else will answer them. You'll be running around the clubhouse with the other girls, wreaking havoc in no time."

"I was afraid to join them."

He rubbed her fingers along his lips. "That was my fault, wasn't it?"

She nodded. "I didn't want to see you if you were avoiding me."

He flattened her hand to his chest. "I'm sorry I was such a doo-doo head. It won't happen again."

Another delightful giggle. "Doo-doo head."

He chuckled. It was a silly word. He had no idea why he'd used it except it seemed appropriate with Addie. It was time to change the subject. "Will you tell me who that man was, Angel?"

She sighed. "Yeah." She pushed herself more upright. "First, can I have some water, please?"

"Of course, Little one." He reluctantly lifted her off his lap and stood her on her feet, holding her hips to make sure she was steady before he stood. He hated breaking the intimate contact, but he also didn't want her to feel crowded.

After tugging the stuffed bear from her grip, he set it on the chair. Taking her hand, he led her to the other side of the room, toward the kitchen area.

"You live here?"

"Yep. This is my apartment."

"Some members have homes in town, though, right?"

"Yes." He lifted her off the floor and sat her on the counter before opening a cabinet and pulling down a pink sippy cup.

He was glad he had one in the apartment and that it was pink. "Every member has at least a room here where they can crash anytime they want. The members with board positions have apartments. Some of us live here full-time."

"You're the secretary, right?"

"Yep."

"So you, like, take notes at the meetings and stuff."

"Exactly."

"Plus, you Daddy all the Little girls, even though they're not yours."

He winked. "You're observant."

She shrugged.

He filled the cup with ice and water, screwed on the top, and handed it to her.

She giggled. "I can drink out of a regular glass, you know. I'm twenty-two years old."

"I'm sure you can, Little one, but when you're Little, you'll use a sippy cup. Plus, it's spillproof, so you can use it even while you're snuggling with Daddy." He lifted her back up, settled her on his hip, and returned to the recliner.

After snagging the stuffie, he slid her around to his front so she was straddling him when he sat. It was intimate and slightly risky, but he wanted to see her close up and face-to-face.

She lifted the cup with one hand, holding the handle on one side of the cup, and took a sip.

He settled the bear between them, reached for her other hand, and brought it to the cup. "Two hands, Angel," he gently commanded, watching her closely.

She shivered, but she obeyed him.

When she lowered the cup between them, she was staring at him again. "You're good at that."

He smiled. "I'm old. I've been around a while."

"How old are you?"

"Forty-four. Twice your age." He watched her face closely.

She didn't flinch. Instead, she sighed, her shoulders dropping. "I guess you do know stuff then, huh?"

He chuckled. "A lot of stuff, especially about how to take
care of a Little girl. Plus, I'm observant enough to know when
that Little girl is being naughty and avoiding my questions."
He lifted a brow.

She drew in a deep breath. "He was my fiancé."

Bear's eyes went wide. "Was?"

She nodded, then lowered her gaze and fiddled with the
front of her sweater. "I, uh, left him at the altar three months
ago."

"Oh." Bear was slightly stunned, but mostly because he
hadn't had a clue what to expect. "Why?"

She lifted her gaze. "Because I don't know him, and I don't
love him."

Apparently, she could continue to shock him. "Then why
were you marrying him?"

"Because my mother wanted me to. She thought the union
would be good for both our families—the optics or something.
I was like a zombie, doing what she wanted me to do for five
years, and I guess I snapped. I was standing in that stupid
bridal room at the church, and I suddenly knew I couldn't go
through with it. There were hundreds of people there. I probably didn't know even ten of them. I didn't even know my
own bridesmaids. I only saw Joseph about a dozen times
before that day. He didn't love me either. I don't know why he
went along with the farce. I never asked him. I never asked
him *anything*. He never even looked me in the eye. And there
we were, about to get married. It was too ridiculous, and I ran
out the side door, begged one of the limo drivers to take me to
the airport, and got on the first flight out. This is where I
ended up."

Bear gently took the cup from Addie and set it on the end
table before clasping both of her hands in his. "I'm proud of
you, Little one."

She gasped. "You're proud of me?" Her voice rose. "I'm an idiot. A weakling. I let my mother boss me around until I was backed into a corner. I was like a walking zombie, I tell you. I embarrassed her and probably Joseph. I'm honestly surprised she hasn't tracked me down and dragged me home yet. I mean, I'm not that hard to find. I used my own information and social security number to register for classes and get jobs, including this one. I'm sure she had a PI on me the entire time. But I didn't really expect Joseph to show up."

"Do you think there's any chance it was a coincidence?"

She shook her head. "No. It's too random. I came here from far away. Also, neither Joseph nor his father has ever even seen a motorcycle up close. There's no way his father owns one. His story was stupid."

Bear chuckled at her exuberance. "Okay. Do you suppose it's possible Joseph just wants to talk to you?"

She shrugged. "I don't know. I panicked. Maybe. But why? And if he did, why would he make up such a ludicrous story and pretend he goes by the name Joe? He's never used that nickname in his life."

"Mmm. Okay. Well, he was dressed like he has money."

Addie rolled her eyes. "That's an understatement. His family is loaded, and…and…so is mine. That's why the merger was important to both my mother and his parents."

Bear cringed. "Merger. That's a terrible word for a marriage."

"That's why I ran. See? But it was cowardly, and I'm embarrassed for not stopping the nonsense sooner. I should've pulled up my big-girl panties, marched into that sanctuary, and told everyone I was calling off the wedding. I shouldn't have let it go that far in the first place. I shouldn't have ever agreed to the farce."

"What's important is that you realized it before it was too late, Angel. You're here now and not in that arranged marriage. Now, you mentioned you haven't been yourself for five years. Did something happen five years ago to change your life?"

"Yeah. My father died."

"I'm so sorry, Little one. That must've been hard. You were only seventeen."

"It was hard. We were close, well, at least much closer than I ever was with my mom. He never would have asked me to marry a man I didn't know, let alone one I didn't love. I miss him. I kind of became a recluse after he died. I stopped going out with friends. I went through the motions of going to college. I graduated. I let my mother plan a wedding. I was in a daze, not making my own choices."

"Wait, you graduated from college?"

"Yes."

"Then why are you taking classes now?"

"Because I want to be an accountant. My mother insisted I get a stupid English degree because it was respectable. She didn't think I needed to get a serious degree that would be useful. She thought aiming for a degree in maths would make me seem too educated and unapproachable. She worried no one would want to marry me if they thought I was too smart."

She kept shocking Bear. Jesus. Her mother was a piece of work. He worried that someday he would find himself face-to-face with this woman, and he would need to keep his cool and make nice for Addie's sake.

"Addie…"

"See?" She sat up taller. "Even my name. My mother only ever called me Adelaine, and she insisted everyone else do so as well. It's such a stuffy name. I always hated it. I tried to get my friends to call me Addie when I was younger, but she caught me and made me write my full name out every day after school until I filled an entire notebook. She told me to stop that nonsense, that she didn't ever want to hear it again. She'd named me Adelaine, and that was my name."

Bear felt every bit of pain and anguish his Little girl must have endured at such a young age. Who treated a child like that? He also made a mental note to never make Addie write lines for punishment. It would likely trigger her. He was glad he'd found out now.

"I'm so sorry, Little one." He brought her palms to his face and kissed first one and then the other, loving the way she shivered when his lips touched her skin. He had another question he needed answered. "Did anyone ever spank you when you were young, Addie?"

She shook her head. "No. I wasn't the sort of kid who got into trouble—other than the name thing. I never talked back to my parents or misbehaved. No one had any reason to punish me."

"Well, that sounds boring." He gave her a big smile, hoping to lighten the mood in the room. His Little girl needed to let loose a bit. Enough serious talk for one night. "No wonder you've been curious about getting together with the other Little girls. I'm sure they've told you about the antics they get up to."

She grinned. "Yes."

"I bet you're also curious about what it would feel like to have your bottom spanked. Surely, that hasn't escaped your notice either." He lifted a brow.

She shrugged, the glint in her eye almost mischievous. "I was kind of wondering what would happen if I joined them and they all got into trouble. Since I don't have a Daddy, what would happen to me?"

"Well, you have a Daddy now, so you don't have to wonder."

Her pretty cheeks turned pink again, and the Little angel squirmed on his lap. She was beyond curious. "I don't really know you that well. Spanking seems like it's kind of…intimate."

"It often is intimate, Little one. You're right. All that matters right now is that you and I start building a relationship together. We'll spend time together. You'll get to know me. Eventually, we'll work up to a time when you trust me enough to spank your naughty bottom, knowing I would never harm you."

Her brow furrowed in thought. "Doesn't a spanking hurt?"

"Yes. And every Little girl is different. Some like a simple swat on the bottom to help them feel Little. That's all the reprimand they need. Others like to be spanked hard until they cry. It helps them let go of all kinds of icky feelings that might be bottled up inside. Littles fall anywhere in between. We'll figure out what you like together when you're ready."

She suddenly threw her arms around his neck and leaned in to hug him tightly.

He slid his hands to her back and held her as close as possible even though her heat was now pressing against his cock. There was no way she couldn't feel it.

When she leaned back, she glanced down between them and winced. "Sorry."

"Never be sorry for pressing against Daddy. It's my pleasure."

"But..."

He pressed two fingers to her lips. "No buts. I will cherish every touch of any part of you against any part of me, and my cock will stay in my pants until you're ready for it to come out."

She nodded. "Okay."

He hadn't even kissed her yet, and already he was so hot for her he thought he might self-combust. He wanted everything from her. Visions of her standing in his bedroom wearing his pink shirt, looking all shy, filled his mind.

He wondered how much experience she had in the bedroom, but he wouldn't ask her right now and risk embarrassing her. She needed to have a fun evening with the other Little girls who were undoubtedly waiting for her in the common area.

They would be the best medicine for a Little girl who needed help keeping her mind off the fact that, for some mysterious reason, her ex-fiancé was snooping around town.

"How about if I take you to meet up with the other Little girls? I know Gabriel has prepared a fun dinner for you, and I bet you're hungry."

"What am I going to do about Joseph?"

"I don't know yet, but you don't need to worry about it tonight. The clubhouse is your safety net. No one can bother you or get to you while you're inside."

"What about when I go home later?"

He shook his head. "Angel, you're not going home," he informed her gently. "I won't pressure you to rush our physical relationship, but I will insist you stay here with me from now on. There's no way I could let you go back to your apartment alone."

"Ever?" Her voice squeaked.

No sense sugarcoating it. "Never, Little one. You're mine."

CHAPTER
EIGHT

ddie's mind was still reeling as Bear held her hand and led her to join the other girls. She felt nervous. Not only was this the first time she was going to spend any length of time with all of them, but they were all aware she'd had a minor meltdown behind the receptionist's desk.

She couldn't help but smile as Bear led her into the common room. It was filled with chaos in the form of six women dressed in frilly party dresses, wrangling a giant pile of blankets. It looked like they were making a fort.

Eden spotted her first. "Yay! You're here." She skipped over and wrapped her arms around Addie, whispering in her ear, "Daddy told us not to talk about what happened earlier, so we won't. We're just going to have fun."

"Thank you," Addie responded when Eden leaned back. "Your dress is so pretty."

Eden beamed. "I have tons of them. We all do. Do you want to borrow one?"

Addie glanced around at everyone again. She did feel like the odd man out since she was still dressed for work in jeans and a thin sweater. "Sure."

Eden grabbed her hand and skipped toward the hallway where the apartments were located.

"*Eden,*" Gabriel admonished. "No running."

"Daddy, I'm not running. I'm skipping."

He groaned. "And where are you skipping to?"

"Our apartment so Addie can borrow one of my dresses."

"Okay, but come right back."

"We will, Daddy."

Addie's adrenaline was pumping as she followed her friend around the corner, coming up short when Eden stopped at the first apartment on the left. Eden hurried straight through and into the master bedroom, where she opened the closet to reveal a row of pretty dresses. "What's your favorite color?"

"Pink," Addie declared. For once in her life, she was going to wear a pink dress, even though it would likely cause her to feel smug toward her mother all evening.

"How about this one?" Eden grabbed a hanger and held up the prettiest dress Addie had ever seen. It was much prettier than the ugly thing she'd worn to her own wedding.

She clapped her hands together. "I love it."

Eden pulled it off the hanger and handed it to her. "You can change in the bathroom."

Addie felt giddy. She hadn't felt giddy in years. Even though her ex-fiancé had shown up a short while ago, she pushed it to the back of her mind. She wasn't going to let anything keep her from having fun tonight.

After quickly removing everything but her bra and panties, she pulled the pink dress over her head. It had spaghetti straps and layers of tulle under pale pink shimmering satin. Her bra was black, and the straps looked silly, plus she couldn't zip it up.

Addie opened the door a crack and peeked out to find Eden leaning against the bed, waiting for her. "Can you help me?"

"Of course." Eden shoved off the mattress and stepped into the bathroom.

"I can't zip it up, but also, my bra looks ridiculous. Do you think I could just take it off?"

"Definitely. A lot of the time, when any of us are in Little space, we don't wear a bra anyway. I'm not wearing one." Eden pulled out the front of her baby blue dress to indicate she was bare beneath.

Addie immediately lowered the front of the dress, popped off her bra, and tugged it free. She giggled as she pulled the pink satin back up over her chest.

"Feels kind of freeing, doesn't it?" Eden asked.

"Very." Addie shivered as her friend zipped up the back. "I feel somehow *more* Little."

"Yep. That happens. Most of the time when I'm here in the clubhouse, Daddy dresses me. He doesn't offer me a bra."

He dresses her… Why did that make Addie's heart race? As she stared at herself in the mirror behind the bathroom door, she went into her head, picturing Bear choosing her clothes and putting them on her. Butterflies danced in her tummy at the thought of standing naked in front of him while he lowered a dress over her head.

Eden giggled. "You should see your face right now."

Addie smiled. "I think I'm aroused by this entire thing," she admitted.

Eden hugged her from the side. "And now you know the appeal of age play. Ready?"

Addie gathered up her clothes and shoes. "Should I just go barefoot? My Converse sneakers would ruin the outfit."

"Barefoot is perfect. We can drop off your clothes in Bear's apartment before we join the others."

"Oh. Right. Okay." He had indicated in no uncertain terms that she would be sleeping in his apartment tonight. It was reasonable that she would leave her clothes there. This was all happening so fast that she felt like she'd slipped into another dimension.

Bear's apartment was the fourth one on the left side of the hallway, and Addie set her pile on the couch before rejoining Eden, who waited for her in the doorway.

"Does anyone lock their doors?"

"Not usually. No one can get into the clubhouse who isn't a member or with a member. Whenever I enter the apartment with Daddy and hear the snick of the lock behind me, I instantly get horny." She covered her mouth as she laughed. "It can only mean one thing."

Addie skipped alongside her friend as they returned to the common area. The other five women were in the process of making a giant blanket fort. Two of the Daddies, Atlas and Talon, were helping.

Addie looked around for Bear and found him setting the table in the kitchen area. He gave her a slow grin, letting his gaze roam up and down her body. Apparently, he liked her clothing selection.

"Okay, Littles." Talon's voice boomed as he reached into the middle of the construction and attached the corner of one of the blankets to the top of a chair. "Dinner first. Gabriel cooked. After dinner, you can hold your secret Littles club meeting in your soundproof fort." He chuckled.

Elizabeth rolled her eyes. "Daddy…"

Talon grabbed her around the waist and kissed the top of her head. "I'm just teasing you, Buttercup. Come eat, then you can play."

Eden and Addie hadn't even joined the fray yet, but Eden took her hand and led her toward the table.

Bear held out a chair for her, leaning in to whisper in her ear as he pushed her up to the table. "You look so pretty, Angel."

She blushed. "Thank you."

Bear picked up her plate. "Gabriel went all out for Little

night. Chicken nuggets, mac and cheese, and veggies with dip. Can I make you a plate?"

She glanced around, noticing all the other Daddies were filling their Littles' plates. "Yes, Sir."

Bear leaned close to her ear again. "Addie, I like the sound of that. I'll like it even better when you're comfortable enough to call me Daddy."

She shivered, partly from his words and partly because his lips tickled her ear.

It was odd watching someone fill her plate. When he was done, he asked if she wanted water, milk, or juice. She chose juice, and he brought her a sippy cup.

Is this how it always is around here? The men doting on the women, cooking and serving them?

It was baffling but also kind of awesome. Her mother had taught her that she would be expected to run her household after she was married and play hostess for Joseph's guests. The idea had never sat well with Addie, but this new world she'd fallen into was the polar opposite.

The women talked while they ate. They seemed to all be in a very Little headspace and didn't break out of it. Their banter was silly and refreshing as they discussed the games they might play that evening or the movies they might watch.

The food was delicious, and when they were done, Addie stood and picked up her plate to take it to the dishwasher.

Bear took it out of her hand. "I've got it, Angel. Go play." He kissed her forehead. It felt so nice when he did that, and she wondered when he might kiss her properly. She was looking forward to finding out how it would feel.

Addie joined the other women, and she quickly fell under their giggling spell as she crawled into the blanket fort. They all sat cross-legged in a circle. Ivy was holding a thick notebook and whispered, "Does anyone need to add anything to the notebook tonight?"

Harper raised her hand and whispered, "Meanie-pants

Daddy has a new enema nozzle in the clinic. It's wider than the last one. Avoid getting your bottoms cleaned out if you can."

Addie gasped and stopped breathing. She was sure her eyes were bugged out of her head.

Eden grabbed her hand. "Maybe we shouldn't have started with that detail. Addie is new to age play. I don't think she's ready for talk about enemas."

Harper winced. "Shoot. Right. Sorry, Addie." She lifted the notebook. "We keep all kinds of secret Little notes in here if you want to look through them, including comparing things that happen to us when one of our Daddies takes us to Doc. He's my Daddy."

Addie leaned into the circle. "You have a clinic in the compound?"

"Yep." Remi nodded. "If you get a fever, expect to be hauled off to the clinic, where you will end up with a thermometer in your bottom."

Addie's breath hitched again. She thought her heart might beat out of her chest. She was crossing into new territory. She'd read about Littles. She'd even read a lot of books in which Littles ended up at the doctor. But each time she found out another aspect of this lifestyle was real, she was shocked all over again.

Even more stunning was that she was squirming. Visions of Bear carrying her into that clinic, pulling her pants down, and holding her bottom open while Doc took her temperature made her palms sweat and her panties wet.

When Addie had left her apartment this morning, she hadn't expected to be in any sort of situation where someone might see her panties, so she'd put on plain cotton panties. Pink, because she'd started buying pink things.

They were simple and boring, and she'd bought them because her mother would never have approved. When she'd lived at home, her mother had insisted she own lingerie sets, with matching panties and bras made of uncomfortable lace that served no purpose whatsoever because not one human ever saw them.

One of the first things Addie had purchased after arriving in town had been plain panties and bras that didn't match at all. Now, she felt kind of weird about it since Bear would undoubtedly see them, perhaps even tonight.

Eden rubbed her back. "Are you okay? We'll change the subject."

Addie shook her head, sending her silky hair flying. "I'm fine. Talk about whatever you normally talk about. I don't want you to censor yourselves just because I'm here."

Carlee narrowed her gaze. "You sure?"

"Positive. I've read books; it's just that I didn't realize people did the things in my fictional romance novels."

Everyone giggled. It was refreshing.

"We do all the things," Harper said, "especially if your Daddy happens to be the club Doc."

Addie was kind of glad that wasn't the case. Surely, the club secretary would not drag her to the clinic to get her temperature taken. Would he?

Addie listened as the rest of the women giggled about nicknames they had for the Daddies and previous shenanigans. Apparently, they'd once hidden in a huge tree behind the clubhouse, and when the Daddies had found them snickering up on the high branches, they'd all gotten spanked.

The more they talked about spanking, trips to see Doc, and all the ways they submitted to their Daddy Doms, the more Addie squirmed. Was she cut out for this lifestyle? She wasn't sure, but her panties were wet, and she kind of wished she'd kept her bra on because her nipples were hard points that kept rubbing against the front of the dress.

"What do you think, Addie?" Eden asked her.

Addie realized she'd gone into her head and hadn't heard

the question. "I'm sorry. I wasn't paying attention. What do I think about what?"

"We were just trying to decide if we should spend the evening being angelic or naughty. We don't want to make you uncomfortable, though. If you're not ready to test out your naughty side, we can behave this evening."

Addie sat straighter. She thought about it for a moment and then grinned. "I never got into trouble as a child. Heck, I never even got into trouble as an adult. I think it's time for me to raise some Cain."

Ivy gasped. "You've never even gotten into trouble as an adult?"

Addie blushed. "Well, I did take off from my own wedding a few months ago."

There was a collective gasp. All eyes were wide.

"What?" Eden asked. "Oh… Was that man out front your fiancé?"

Addie nodded. She didn't feel nearly as upset by the events now that a few hours had passed. She thought she could talk about it, and who else would she tell but these six women who had taken her in as one of their friends?

She nodded. "I don't know what he's doing here in town, but I have to assume he knows I'm here. He must be looking for me."

"Are you married to him?" Carlee asked. "Or did you leave him standing at the altar?"

"I left him at the altar, kicked off my stupid shoes, and ran out a side door. I conned a limo driver into taking me to the airport. The first flight out was to here, so I took it."

Harper covered her gasp with a hand over her mouth. "That's so…brave."

Addie winced. "I think I was a coward. I should've faced my mother and told her I didn't want to marry Joseph a long time ago. I was dragging through my life as though I'd been floating along next to my body."

Elizabeth frowned. "Why would you tell your *mother* you didn't want to marry your fiancé? Why wouldn't you tell *him*?"

The laugh that bubbled out of Addie's throat was cathartic. Now that she was finally discussing the saga out loud instead of in her head, it all seemed so ridiculous. "I don't even know him very well. We only met about a dozen times. I've never even been alone with him."

All the girls gasped again.

"Seriously?" Eden's voice rose. "It was like an arranged marriage?"

Addie nodded. "Basically. My mother and Joseph's parents thought it would be a good social move to unite our families. It was just expected of me."

"Do you think Joseph was mad, and that's why he's looking for you?"

"I don't know. I seriously don't know enough about him to know what his moods might be. I don't even know if he's mild-mannered or might be fuming angry."

Eden leaned in closer, eyes wide. "It's like a scene out of a movie. I wish I could've been there to see you running toward the limo, holding your dress up. Was it all poufy? Did it stick out the car door when you slammed it?"

Addie started laughing so hard that tears ran down her cheeks. When she was finally able to catch her breath, she shook her head. "No. Worse. I didn't even get to pick the dress. If I had picked it, it would've been pale pink with delicate lace sewn into it. It would have had layers of tulle under it."

"Kind of like the one you're wearing tonight, only long," Remi said, pointing at Addie's dress.

"Yes. Instead, it was this ugly skintight satin that looked like it belonged on a model. I'm no model. I hated it. It was just one more thing that helped me make up my mind at the last second. I was staring at myself in the mirror in the bride's room, and I hated the woman I was looking at. She was weak and stupid. She needed to find her spine. I left her there and never looked back."

Eden grabbed her hand. "We're so proud of you."

"Yeah," Ivy agreed, "and whatever your ex is doing here, I'm sure the Daddies will figure it out and make sure you're safe."

Safe... Was Addie unsafe? She had no idea. She couldn't picture Joseph being violent. She'd never seen him raise his voice or even utter an opinion about anything.

It bothered her that he'd obviously come to the shop under a false pretense. There was no way he or his father owned a beat-up old bike, and he'd never once gone by the nickname Joe. That meant he'd known she was working here, and he'd come to find her.

Addie shuddered before shaking the fear from her mind. Tonight was all about new friends and new experiences. She wouldn't let Joseph's appearance in town ruin her night.

Pasting on a smile, she said, "Let's do something naughty. I could use the distraction."

Everyone grinned, and they all scooted closer together, leaned in, and whispered.

"Here's the plan..." Ivy began.

CHAPTER
NINE

"Do they think we can't hear them?" Faust asked, chuckling.

Bear shook his head in disbelief, but he couldn't stop grinning. For the first time since he'd joined the MC, one of the Little girls plotting inside the blanket fort was his.

His heart was full, and his chest was tight with the knowledge. He definitely had a lot of shit to work through to get his head on straight. He hadn't suddenly forgotten Valerie and the things she'd said to him. He would need to work that shit out of his system if he was ever going to have a life with Adelaine.

He glanced at Gabriel, the club chaplain, knowing he should probably talk to him. Gabriel was a great listener, and Bear knew he'd provided excellent advice to every one of the club members at one point or another.

Everyone except Bear. Bear had always kept his past bottled up inside, insisting he was fine and didn't need anyone prying into his previous life. And he had been fine until he'd walked into the shop's reception area and set his gaze on the angel who was absolutely his Little girl.

He'd remained pigheaded for two more weeks before finally pulling his head out of his ass today and facing the truth. How had he ever thought he could ignore the magnetic pull toward her?

He loved that she'd confided in the other Littles about her ex and his appearance in town. It was saying something that she was comfortable enough to share with them.

He had winced and held his breath when the girls had first entered the fort and launched right into a discussion about enemas and thermometers, but she'd somehow taken things in stride. At least she hadn't clambered out of the fort and run for the front door.

When the girls had conspired to do something naughty, he'd wondered how Addie might feel about joining it, and he'd been pleased when she'd agreed.

"What on Earth do you suppose they're plotting?" Steele whispered to the huddled group.

Everyone shrugged. So far, they could only hear murmured giggles. Most of the time, the Littles weren't quiet enough to hide whatever they did in their "private" club meetings, probably because they didn't actually care if their Daddies knew what they were discussing. They made a huge production about being secretive, but it never ended up happening that way.

Bear turned his head to one side, trying to listen closer. There was a lot of giggling and then voices that didn't belong to the girls. What the heck?

Atlas started chuckling with a hand over his mouth. "They took a tablet in."

"Is that…moaning?" Talon asked.

Bear's chest heaved from suppressed laughter. They were watching porn. The naughty Little stinkers thought they could watch porn and get away with it? "Don't you have parental controls on that tablet?" he asked Kade, knowing Kade was the one who'd purchased the tablet for the Littles and had left it in the library for them to use.

"Yep, but Remi is sly. She always figures out my password."

Bear kept chuckling under his breath. A five-year-old could hack into a tablet to watch anything they wanted. Everyone knew that. Bear loved that Addie was in there, giggling with the rest of them. He already recognized the specific sound of her voice and knew every time he heard the soft tinkle of laughter.

"What's it called?" Addie whispered loudly.

"A Tantra chair," Harper told her.

Doc rolled his eyes and ran a hand down his face. He motioned for all the men to lean in and explained that Harper had seen one in a magazine and had asked him about it earlier in the day.

Bear covered his mouth. It was growing more difficult to suppress outward laughter. He could picture the seven of them leaning over that tablet, looking at the ergonomic S-curved lounge chair. Except there was no way they were simply looking at design features. These naughty girls were watching porn.

The whispering grew louder.

"Oh! Can someone really do that?"

"Is she upside down?"

"How did she get her legs like that?"

"Now, that's a cool position. It would be a lot more comfortable to lean over the tall end of that Tantra chair than the back of the couch."

"Remi!"

"What? Like you don't take it from behind sometimes. *Paaalease.*"

"Oh my God. I've never seen a cock that large before in my life."

Bear jerked to attention. So did the rest of the men.

"That's it. I think fun time is over," Kade declared. He was the first to reach the fort, and he yanked the top of it away so fast that the Littles never had a chance to cover their tablet.

All seven of them gasped, tipping their heads back. Lying on the floor in between the huddle was the tablet, and the video they'd been watching was an extremely graphic X-rated scene.

Kade leaned in and snatched up the tablet. "Looks like some naughty girls broke through the parental controls on this device. I believe your electronic privileges need to be revoked until further notice."

"Daddy!" Remi shouted. "We were just looking up furniture."

It was seriously tough not to laugh. For months, as six other members of the MC met their perfect Littles and brought them into the fold, Bear had watched these antics from the sidelines. He'd laughed with the rest of them on many occasions, but he'd never been directly involved. Not until tonight.

It felt good. The look on Addie's face was precious. Since this was her first night joining in the shenanigans, she had no real idea about what was coming, but her cheeks were flushed pink, and she kept licking her lips.

Kade turned off the video and set the tablet on a high shelf in the common room before crossing his arms and glaring at all the Littles.

"Sorry, Daddy," Remi said, the first to pull her tail between her legs.

A chorus of sorries followed.

Even though Addie looked shell-shocked, she also managed to mutter an apology.

Bear noticed it was Ivy who snatched up the "private" notebook and ran over to "hide" it behind some other books in the library.

In no time at all, every Little was being led from the room by her Daddy.

Bear wasn't certain what Addie might need from him, but he intended to find out. "Come, Little one."

She rose on shaky legs and followed him all the way to his apartment—except it wasn't his anymore. It was theirs. From now on, he intended for Addie to spend most of her time in this apartment, especially at night.

When he shut and locked the door, she gasped. Her entire body stiffened as she backed up. It was…odd.

"Addie?" He remained just inside the room, leaning against the door, wondering what had spooked her. "You okay?"

She nodded slowly. Her gaze was on the knob, and she licked her lips.

He glanced at the knob. "Do you want me to leave the door open?" He would if it made her feel more comfortable. She hadn't been nearly this skittish earlier when he'd brought her to the apartment, but she'd been pretty distraught at the time. It was possible she was nervous about being alone with him.

"No, Sir. It's fine."

"It doesn't seem fine. You know I would never do anything you didn't consent to, right, Angel?" It occurred to him she was probably worried about being spanked.

She gave a slow nod. Her eyes were wide, and her hands were clasped behind her back. He noticed the clothes she'd changed out of were in a pile on the end of the couch. She must have brought them here after changing in Eden's apartment.

"Tell me why you're so nervous, Addie. I would never discipline you in any way without your consent and some discussion. If you're not ready for me to spank you, that's fine."

"Okay." She relaxed, her shoulders lowering.

Bear slowly made his way to the couch and sat in the middle. "Come here, Angel," he encouraged.

She shuffled toward him.

He set his hands on her hips and met her eye-to-eye. "I mean it, Addie. I may be certain I'm your Daddy, but I will not spank you just because that's what the other Daddies might be doing right now. This is your first night here. I'm so glad you felt comfortable enough to join the other girls and have some fun, but you and I haven't discussed rules and expectations yet, so I wouldn't expect you to lean over my lap yet, either, okay?"

She nodded again. "I don't care if you spank me," she whispered.

He frowned. "Then what's upsetting you?"

"Nothing, really. It's just that Eden said the only time her Daddy locks the door is when they, uh…"

Ahh. "When they have sex."

"Yes." Her cheeks turned bright red. "I don't think I'm quite ready to do that yet. Is that okay?"

"Of course." He pulled her closer. "Addie, you are my life. I know your head is spinning, and it's hard to grasp what I'm telling you, but you're mine. My Little girl. It's my job to make sure you're happy. We will absolutely not have sex until you're certain beyond a shadow of a doubt it's what you want."

She was trembling, but she nodded. "Okay."

She seemed inordinately nervous about sex, and he suddenly wondered if someone had touched her inappropriately. Perhaps Joseph? "Has anyone ever touched you without your permission, Angel?"

"No, Sir." She shook her head vehemently.

"I don't just mean sex itself, Addie. Maybe someone groped you or grabbed your breasts or your pussy without your permission?"

She leaned in closer to him and set her forehead against his chest. "No, Daddy."

His heart lurched. She'd called him Daddy.

He rubbed her back, still kind of confused by her reaction to the locked door.

Finally, she lifted her head and met his gaze. "No one has touched me with or without my permission, Daddy."

His heart stopped. Oh. *Ohhh.* No wonder she'd panicked when he'd locked the door. Jesus. And…well, holy mother.

It hadn't seemed possible for her face to grow any redder, but it did, and his brave girl did not look away, so he didn't either.

"Thank you for telling me, Addie." He moved his hands to her biceps and rubbed up and down. "We will take all the time in the world you need to grow into a physical relationship, okay?"

She nodded. "Thank you."

Another thought had him twisted in a knot. "Is that even something you're interested in, Angel?"

Her eyes went wide. "Of course." Her gaze roamed up and down his body. "You're…" She swallowed.

"I'm what?" He forced himself not to grin.

"So sexy and built and…stuff."

"Stuff?" he teased.

She swatted at his shoulder playfully. "Daddy…"

He pulled her in close again, hugging her. "That word coming from your lips is the sweetest thing I've ever heard. Say it again."

"Silly."

"Please?"

"Daddy…"

He sighed. "Yeah, just like that." He leaned her back. "Now, let's get a few things straight. I don't care how much time you need before you're ready for Daddy to be naked in front of you, but I do need to be sure you have those kinds of feelings for me so I'll know we're on the same page."

"I do." She shifted her weight back and forth. "I've never met anyone who made my tummy feel like you do."

"Good. What about your pussy. Is it tingly and wet?"

She nodded. "Yes. My panties are soaked," she admitted.

"Good. The rest will come."

"Are you going to spank me now?" she asked, changing the subject.

"Do you want me to, Angel?"

"Yes, because all the other Littles are getting spanked right now. They told me they do naughty things like we did tonight on purpose because they all like it when they get spanked."

"That's true, but it doesn't mean you have to receive a spanking if you're not ready." He lifted her and set her on one knee with her legs dangling between his. "Let me tell you a few things."

"Okay."

"When I spank you, it will always be on your bare bottom. I want to be able to see how your skin is reacting to my swats. It's important that I always pay close attention so that I never strike you too hard. A spanking should leave a lasting sting that lingers for a few hours but not into the next day."

"Okay," she muttered quietly.

"Another thing. Do you know why all the Littles want to get spanked, Addie?"

She shook her pretty head, her hair flying.

"There are a few reasons. One of them is that spankings help Little girls purge themselves of icky thoughts. A spanking can be freeing. The pain washes away the naughty behavior."

Her brows were furrowed. It was a difficult concept to understand until someone experienced it.

"You'll see." He patted her thighs. "But there's another reason the Littles are so eager to end up over their Daddies' knees. It's titillating."

"Oh." She didn't look too stunned. In fact, she squirmed on his lap, her thigh coming precariously close to his cock.

"You already assumed that, didn't you, Angel?" He tucked a lock of hair behind her ear.

"I guess."

"Because the thought of lying across my lap while I swat your naughty bottom makes you squirm."

"Yes, Sir," she whispered. At least she was honest.

"Sometimes, when Daddies are finished spanking their Little girls, they reach between their legs and touch their pussies, letting them come."

Addie swallowed. A shudder shook her entire frame. Adorable.

"Sometimes, Daddies do not let their Littles come. Sometimes, they make them squirm and leave them without the release they crave, especially if they were really naughty and broke a rule involving their safety."

Addie bravely held his gaze. "Okay."

He needed to know something else before they continued. "Have you had an orgasm before, Addie?"

Her breath hitched, and for a moment, he didn't think she would answer. Finally, she nodded.

"Okay. I only ask so I'll know what to expect when I'm touching you. I assume, since no one else has touched you, that you've masturbated and given yourself pleasure, right?"

"Yes, Daddy." Her voice was so soft.

It was selfish of him to ask his next question, but he did it anyway. "Have you masturbated since we met?"

Damn, but her cheeks were fucking sexy. And she didn't need to answer him. He could see her response on her face and in her eyes.

She licked her lips slowly and responded, though. "Yes, Daddy. I've *only* done it since we met."

Fuck. Me.

Could his cock get any bigger?

He tried to control his breathing as he cupped her face. "You never had an orgasm until two weeks ago?"

"No, Sir. I never even tried."

This time, it was Bear who licked his lips. "Do you do it with your fingers, Little one?" He wanted every fucking detail.

He wanted to go back in time and watch. Every time she'd touched herself, she'd been thinking of him. He felt like he could fly to the moon.

"Yes, Sir," she whispered. She squirmed again. She was embarrassed to talk about this, but it also made her horny.

Bear wanted to pause this moment and commit it to memory for the rest of his life.

CHAPTER
TEN

A ddie was embarrassed, but at the same time, she was so aroused she thought she might come. If she rubbed her legs together hard enough, she could orgasm without touching herself.

The entire evening, her arousal had been building. Something about age play was so titillating that she couldn't stop thinking about what it would be like to have sex. Sex with Bear.

She hated how she'd reacted to the locked door. She felt bad about that. It was just that even though she wanted him, she was also nervous about her first time. She was relieved that he'd insisted they wait until she was ready.

On the other hand, he'd discussed spanking and masturbation with her so matter-of-factly that she felt like she might as well have been naked and spread open. That's how aroused she was.

"How often have you touched yourself in the past two weeks, Angel?" His voice was soft and caring, but the question was so very private and personal. So invasive. It was exactly what she would expect from a Daddy, and honestly, she might have been disappointed if he wasn't forcing her to tell him such intimate details about her sexual experiences.

Daddy cupped her face and tipped her head back, forcing her to look him in the eye again. "Addie, tell Daddy. Did you touch your pussy every night?"

She nodded. If her face got any hotter, she would end up in Doc's clinic with a thermometer in her bottom. And why did she have to go and think something like that?

"Did you come every time, Angel?"

"Yes, Daddy," she murmured.

"Did you only stroke your clit, or did you push your fingers up inside your tight little pussy?"

She was panting. She was going to come on his lap, and then she would be mortified. "Daddy…"

He stroked her lip with his thumb. "Tell Daddy."

"Why?"

He gave her a slight smile. "Because it's making you so hot that your pussy is leaking through your panties and soaking Daddy's jeans. Because your nipples are so tight and hard, I can see them poking against your dress."

He was right. Darn him.

Her lip trembled against his thumb, and she realized something else. She wasn't the only one aroused. His erection was hard and pressing against her thigh. He might have been asking her all these questions to make her horny, but it was having the same effect on him.

She decided to turn the table. She'd never been so bold in her life, but this man *was* her life now. She knew it in her soul, even if her brain wasn't ready to fully accept it yet.

Holding his gaze, she licked the tip of his thumb. "The first orgasm I had was the night after I met you. I couldn't sleep. I kept thinking about you. You were so stern and tall and broad. I wanted to run my hands through your beard and thick hair. I was tossing and turning until I finally took my panties off and touched myself. I planted my heels wide and rubbed my clit until I came."

Bear looked like he might pass out, which made Addie feel oddly powerful. She suspected he was going to keep her on edge with arousal often. It was only fair that she showed him she could do the same thing.

She didn't even know who she was. She'd never been this bold, but she kept going. "The next night, I pushed my fingers inside my channel and learned that was even better. Do you want to know what I did next?"

He slowly smiled and narrowed his gaze. "Yes, naughty girl. Tell Daddy what you did next."

"I ordered a vibrator. It came the next day. It's probably nowhere near as thick as you, but it's pink, and it rotates inside me, and it has these little ears that rub against my clit. When I close my eyes and think of the way you looked at me that first day, I can come in two minutes."

His smile grew. "You are such a naughty girl." He lifted her fingers and brought them to his lips to kiss them.

"Why?" she asked, feigning innocence. "Lots of women have vibrators and use them regularly. I figure at twenty-two, I'm way behind my peers. I thought I should make up for lost time."

Daddy chuckled. "What happened to the innocent Little girl with the halo of light around her head that first day I saw you?"

She shrugged. "You ruined her."

His face sobered, and he took a deep breath. "Fuck me. You are full of surprises. And the reason I said you were naughty isn't because you touched yourself, Angel; it's because you just used that information to tease your Daddy on purpose."

"Weren't you teasing me on purpose by begging me to tell you?" she pointed out.

He chuckled. "Yes."

"Are we even?"

"Not even close, Little girl. Not even close."

She gave him a pout, pushing her bottom lip out. "Why not?"

"Because I'm the Daddy. I'm the one who's going to flip you over, pull those wet panties off your body, and spank your bottom until you're clear about who the Daddy is." He lifted a brow.

Her breath hitched. She wanted that. She really did. But what if they got carried away? She might have been bold enough to tell him about her experiences with a vibrator, but she wasn't sure she was ready to take him into her body. That part kind of freaked her out.

"Are you ready for that, Angel?"

"We aren't going to have sex?"

"No, Little one. You have my word. My pants will stay on my body. I will not change my mind even if you ask me to."

"Okay."

"Just one more question before I begin. Do you want Daddy to make you come?"

She couldn't deny that. "Yes, Daddy." He might not even have to touch her for her to come. She was almost there now.

He kissed her fingers again. "Good choice because the first rule that's going on the top of your list is no more touching yourself without permission."

She gasped. *What?*

"You heard me. Keep your fingers away from your pussy from now on. If you're horny and you need to come, you tell Daddy. If I decide you deserve an orgasm, I can either do it for you or watch you do it. You aren't permitted to rub yourself to orgasm without me from now on."

She stared at him, eyes wide, mouth hanging open. When she could finally close it, she said, "How would you know?"

He smiled so wide that she shivered. "Because you'll never have an opportunity, Angel."

"You can't watch me all the time, Daddy."

"Sure I can. When you're in our bed, I'll be in it with you."

She smirked, thinking there was no way he could be with her *all* the time. "I could still do it in the shower or even in the bathroom. In fact, there's a fantastic new knob on the bathroom door at the back of the reception area. It locks and everything," she taunted.

He chuckled. "Angel, you will not be bathing alone, and if I need to, I don't mind watching you pee. Do I need to put a lock on the outside of that bathroom in the shop so you have to call me to get the key to open it?"

She gasped. He wouldn't.

"Try me." His eyes danced with mirth.

He was serious.

"Are you going to touch yourself?"

She sighed in defeat. "No, Sir."

"I didn't think so. I'm not worried. I bet you've never told a lie in your life. You'd never be able to keep a straight face when I ask you if your fingers have been inside your pussy."

"Meanie."

He laughed hard. "The other Littles have already rubbed off on you. Apparently, you're going to fit in just fine." He stroked her lip again, bringing her arousal back. Why was that simple act so sexy? "Are you ready for your first spanking?"

"Yes, Sir."

"Good girl." He stood her on her feet, lifted her dress, and hooked his fingers into her panties to pull them down her legs.

She shivered. This was the closest she'd ever been with a man.

Bear brought them to his nose and inhaled her scent. "Mmm. You smell so good, and these panties are soaked."

She flushed. No denying the fact.

He set them on the pile with the rest of her clothes and then surprised her by pulling her between his legs. He slid his hands up her arms until he cupped her neck and cheeks. "I'd like to kiss you first. May I?"

"Yes." She wanted that more than anything.

His thumbs stroked her lips again. "Has anyone kissed you before, Angel?"

"No, Daddy," she murmured.

"Does that embarrass you?"

"A little. I'm kind of old to have never been kissed, but I never met anyone I wanted to do that with. Certainly not my fiancé. Besides, he never acted like he wanted to either." So why was he in town?

She shook thoughts of Joseph from her mind. He didn't belong in this room with this man who looked her in the eyes and made her feel things for the first time in her life.

"I want to, Angel."

She smiled.

He slowly lowered his lips to her. The first contact was soft and gentle as he brushed his lips across hers. And then he angled his head slightly to one side and deepened the connection.

Addie melted against him. This was what she'd always imagined. This was why she'd never kissed a boy in school. She'd wanted fireworks and wouldn't accept anything less.

Bear gave her fireworks. He gave her so much more.

She leaned closer to him, whimpering as he nibbled around her lips before licking the seam and swiping his tongue into her mouth. Her whimper switched to a low moan as the kiss deepened. She lost all sense of time and space, consumed by this man who worshipped her and showed her what a kiss should be like.

When he finally broke the connection, she was panting. She licked her swollen, wet lips. "Oh."

He grinned. "I'm not sorry that all your kisses will be mine."

"Me neither."

Bear guided her around to one side of his lap, lifted her, and settled her across his knees.

She held her breath as he slid her pink dress up her back, exposing her butt.

"Tuck your hands up under your head, Angel."

She did as he ordered.

"Good girl." He pushed the dress higher, settled one hand on the small of her back, and rubbed her thighs with the other. "Spread your legs a few inches, Addie. I don't want you to squeeze them together while I spank you."

Did he have any idea how close she was to an orgasm? Every time he commanded her to do something else in his deep Daddy voice, her arousal grew. She was soaking wet, and her breasts felt heavy as they pressed against the front of the dress.

She didn't think she'd ever be able to disobey him because every time she followed his orders, he praised her, and she loved that feeling. As soon as she parted her knees, he did so again. "Such a good girl. Now, I'm going to spank your bottom. It might feel strange at first. I'll start gently and warm you up. Give it a chance, but if you don't like it, I'll stop."

It calmed her to know he wouldn't do anything she didn't like. It was confusing, though, because she couldn't imagine she was going to like being spanked. That was hard to grasp.

Littles in books enjoyed it, though, and so did all the Littles she'd met here at the MC. So maybe he would surprise her.

The first swat made her breath hitch, mostly because it was shocking. The second one wasn't quite as jarring. By the third, she was more relaxed across his thighs, letting herself focus on the rhythm.

After a few more, he paused and rubbed her heated skin. "How do you feel, Addie?"

"I'm not sure," she murmured.

"May I continue?"

"Yes, Sir."

Her mind drifted as he spanked her harder, every slap echoing in the room and sending her deeper and deeper into an oddly blissful place. Her skin tingled and began to burn but in a good way. She started to understand.

Bear lowered his focus to her thighs and worked his way back up. When he hit the junction of her butt cheeks with her thighs, a rush of arousal leaked out of her, and she moaned. Unable to keep from squeezing her thighs together, she nearly came.

Daddy patted the back of her thighs. "Legs, Addie. Open your knees."

She shook her head and held her breath. She couldn't. If she did, she would orgasm. It would be mortifying.

"Spread your thighs, naughty girl," he demanded in that calm, gentle voice of his.

When she finally thought she could control herself, she inched them apart, but she was still holding her breath.

Bear slid his fingers along the inside of her thighs. "May I touch your pussy, Angel?"

She sucked in a breath and nodded. She needed him to touch her. At least then, it wouldn't be so embarrassing when she came.

"You're so sensitive. The sexiest Little I've ever seen. I want to make you feel good."

"Please…" she begged. She couldn't keep from squirming, or maybe she was just trembling so violently that it seemed like she was wiggling.

The moment his fingers grazed her swollen, wet folds, she moaned.

"That's my good girl. You did so well taking your first spanking. Let Daddy make it feel good." With his hand between her thighs, she was forced to spread them wider, and she willed him to apply more pressure.

That wasn't his plan, though. Instead, he teased her folds, barely stroking them before he finally dipped one finger between her labia and dragged the wetness down to her clit.

Addie lifted her face and cried out. Her body convulsed

with an orgasm more powerful than any she'd given herself in the past two weeks.

And he was barely touching her. One tap to her clit was all it had taken.

Her pussy throbbed as she tried to catch her breath, and it wasn't until she started to descend that Bear finally applied pressure to her clit. Anticipating that she might lurch off his lap, he secured her with a firm grip on her lower back, keeping her in place while he drove her mad.

In seconds she was flying again, soaring above her body, all of her focus on the way he rubbed her clit, and then he pinched it. Waves of her second release made her vision blur. She couldn't breathe. The moment was so intense that it shadowed over the first orgasm.

The moment she flinched from over-stimulation, Daddy removed his fingers. He gently rolled her over and cradled her in his arms. Lifting her higher against his chest, he kissed her forehead and then rained kisses all over her face until he met her lips and slowed the frenzy with a deep, powerful collision of lips and tongues and moans.

Addie was drained, completely sated, and lying limp in her Daddy's arms. Panting, unable to focus, she lacked certainty about whether or not she was right-side up or upside down.

Daddy had her, though. He held her together, cradling her tightly and keeping her from falling apart.

As she slowly came back into her body, she was grinning. She still had on the poufy dress, and really, they hadn't done anything earth-shattering. They hadn't had sex. Daddy was fully dressed. He'd barely touched her. She was certain his spanking had been mild compared to what he was capable of, and the way he'd touched her had been brief and external.

She grabbed his neck when he rose from the couch, holding on as he carried her into the bedroom. His lips came to her ear. "Time for bed, Angel. Do you want to take a bath first?"

She shook her head. "Too tired." She was still trembling.

"Okay." He lowered her to the edge of the bed. "Can you sit up for me?"

She managed to find her balance and sat obediently.

He lowered the zipper down the back of the dress. "Arms up."

Without questioning him, she lifted her arms, shivering a moment later as the dress was whisked over her head. Before she could contemplate the fact that she was sitting naked on his bed, he pulled a T-shirt over her head.

She gasped when he picked her back up, finally opening her eyes a bit more. The next thing she knew, she was sitting on the bathroom counter, and Daddy was opening a new pink toothbrush.

She watched his every move, mesmerized and still dazed from two orgasms. He put toothpaste on the brush and held it up to her mouth. "Open."

He was going to brush her teeth? She didn't argue. She opened her mouth and let him take care of this simple, everyday task.

When he was satisfied, he held her hair back and guided her to lean over the sink. "Spit, Little one." He then gave her a cup of water. "Rinse."

She was like a robot, following instructions. As soon as she rinsed, he wiped her mouth, scooped her up, and turned around to sit her on the toilet. This woke her up all the way. She tipped her head back to look at him.

He cupped her face. "Are you steady enough to potty if I step out of the room?"

"Yes, Sir." She'd find a way. Why was she so dazed?

He left her alone, but he didn't shut the door all the way, and the moment she flushed, he was back, guiding her to the sink before washing her hands.

Addie's heart beat rapidly as he helped her back into the bedroom. The covers were pulled back. He lifted her and settled her in the middle, tucking the covers around her.

Finally, he snagged something from the nightstand and held it up.

She grinned and reached for the stuffie. "Bear."

He chuckled. "Bear? I think he needs a better name than that. I'm Bear."

She shook her head. "You're Daddy. He's Bear." She pulled him under the covers and snuggled him in against her.

Her Daddy was smiling broadly as he leaned over and kissed her forehead. "Sleep, Angel."

"Aren't you going to join me?"

He patted her tummy. "I'm going to take a shower first, and then I'll sleep on the couch."

She frowned. "You can't do that. It's not as long as you. I'm in your bed."

He brushed a lock of hair from her face. "You're in *our* bed, Angel. It's not just mine anymore."

"If it's ours, then you should be in it, too."

He searched her gaze.

"Please?"

"If you're sure you're comfortable with that plan."

"I am. I need you here in case I have a nightmare or wake up confused or scared." She was laying it on thick, including batting her eyelashes. Now that the orgasmic rush was fading, she was sliding back into her Little space.

The sound of her Daddy laughing made her tummy flutter. "I'll join you after I shower, naughty girl. Sleep."

She let her gaze roam down to the front of his jeans. His erection was obvious and huge. She narrowed her eyes and shifted her attention to his face. "Why do I bet there's a double standard between us?"

He rolled his eyes and dropped his palms onto the mattress, leaning over her. "Because there is. You're going to stay right here and keep your naughty fingers above the covers."

"But you said I can't masturbate in the shower," she taunted, feeling friskier by the moment.

The humor on his face wrinkled his eyes. "I didn't say that. I said you can't masturbate in the shower without permission and only if I'm watching."

"Then I should get to watch you, too." She wasn't ready for him to enter her tight channel yet, but she sure would like a front-row seat while he stroked himself, and she was smart enough to know that's exactly what was going to happen.

"Nope. Not this time. Double standard." He picked up her fingers and brought them to his nose, inhaling slowly. "These naughty fingers smell like the soap I just washed them with." It was an odd thing to say, but as he padded toward the bathroom, he looked over his shoulder. "Make sure that's still what they smell like when I come back."

Addie's eyes went wide as he disappeared. *Meanie.*

She stared at the door, which he left ajar, and tried to listen, but once he turned on the water, all she could hear was the spray. Darn. She really did wish she was in there watching, and the thought made it hard to settle her mind and go to sleep.

CHAPTER
ELEVEN

Bear woke up to the feel of silky hair against his cheek, the scent of his Little girl filling his nostrils, and the sound of her breathing as she squirmed in his arms.

"Too hot, Daddy." She pushed against the arm he had wrapped around her.

When he'd joined her in bed, she'd been out cold. She'd been angelic, even in sleep. He'd spent some time ordering a few things for delivery before sliding in with her and pulling her into his arms, and that's the position they were still in now.

After kissing her temple, he squeezed her tighter.

"Need to pee," she grumbled, shoving at his arm again.

He finally released her, loving the fact that as she slid off the side of the bed, the T-shirt rose to give him a view of her perfect ass.

He rolled the other direction and propped up on his elbow to watch her rush past him. "Leave the door open, Angel."

She grabbed the doorframe and twisted around to look at him, eyes wide. "Daddy…"

He lifted a brow, forcing his face to remain stern.

She sighed as she slid into the bathroom. She pulled the

door almost closed, leaving a millimeter of space, which made him chuckle.

He listened as she peed and then washed her hands.

When she returned, he reached out for her from his side of the bed.

"So bossy," she murmured.

"Yep." He leaned over, grabbed her by the waist, and hauled her up on top of him, rolling to his back so that she ended up straddling him. It was intentional. He was only wearing a pair of cotton shorts. Now, her pussy was against his stomach.

"Daddy..." She tried to slide over him, but he held her steady by the hips. Fuck, but she was beautiful. She had the kind of silky hair that always looked like it had been recently brushed to a shine. It was hanging all around her, the length of it falling over her shoulders to dance across his chest.

"Stay still, Little one."

"But..." Her breath hitched as she attempted to move again, which caused her to rub her wet heat against his stomach.

"You can either hold still or keep squirming. I don't mind if you want to rub against me until you come. I have the perfect seat for the show."

She gasped and stopped moving, her pretty cheeks turning pink with embarrassment. He would be perfectly happy if she never lost the shocked innocence that led her to feel embarrassed.

"I need to get to work, and I don't have anything to wear. I'll have to go home."

He shook his head. "You're not leaving the compound for any reason—not until we know why your ex is in town and what he wants. Understood?"

"But I need clothes and some things."

He lifted a brow. "Some things? You mean like a pink rabbit vibrator?" he joked. She was so fun to tease.

The naughty girl rocked her pussy against his abs and sat tall, crossing her arms. "Apparently, I don't need that vibrator anymore." She shrugged. "I probably wore it out anyway."

He laughed. "Oh, Addie, you naughty girl. In two weeks? I don't think anyone can wear out a vibrator in two weeks."

She shrugged as though she'd made her best attempt to wear that vibrator out. She even lifted one hand to pretend to check her nails.

Bear slid his hands under her T-shirt and moved them up until his thumbs rested against the undersides of her breasts. That got her attention. She didn't ask him to stop or push him away. Instead, she arched into him as her mouth fell open.

She was the most sensual creature in the world and all his.

"I'll go to your apartment and get whatever you need. You'll stay here until I get back."

"I can't do that. I have to get to work."

"You're not going to work until I get back, Angel. For now, I don't want you anywhere near the reception area without me."

Her eyes widened. "You can't sit up front with me all day. That's silly."

"Sure, I can, and I will."

"Don't you have a job?" Her head cocked to one side. "I've never known you to go anywhere. Do you get paid to be the club secretary?"

Bear drew in a long breath. *You have to tell her. Do it now.*

Valerie's parting words rang in his head.

Word of advice. Next time you meet a woman you like, don't tell her you have any money. That's the only way you'll know if she authentically cares about you.

Bear shook Valerie's voice from his head. She had no part in his life now. She was long gone. Addie was not Valerie.

Addie must have sensed he'd grown serious because she stopped rocking against him and set her hands on his shoulders, leaning forward, bracing herself, holding his gaze with furrowed brows. "Daddy?"

Tell her.

"Remember how I was telling you about a woman I dated a long time ago and how she hurt me?"

Addie nodded.

"Her name was Valerie."

"You said she pretended to be Little."

Bear nodded. "Yeah." He rubbed her back, trying to find the words.

"Why did she do that, Daddy?"

Bear swallowed. "Because she thought she would have a cushy life with me, and she believed she could pretend to be whatever I wanted."

Addie angled her head to one side, confusion written all over her face.

"I don't work because I don't have to, Addie. I prefer to help everyone around me and make sure my MC family has what they need. That includes you now."

She blinked. "You mean you have money?"

"Yes, Angel." He let that sink in for a minute. "I didn't earn it. My grandfather was wealthy. When my parents passed, I inherited a large sum from the estate."

She slid off him and pulled her shirt under her bottom as she crossed her legs next to him. She didn't turn away, though. "I was raised with money."

"I gathered that." He turned onto his side, facing her, setting his hand on her hip.

"I hate money," she said emphatically.

Her response was rather unexpected, but he shouldn't have been surprised.

"I hate what it does to people. I hate how it rules their lives. My mother cares about nothing but her social standing in society, and that includes me, who I marry, and what people think about me. I ran from that."

"I know you did, Angel." There was a ball of nerves in his throat, but he had to let her process.

"You don't act like that."

"No, Addie, I don't. I never will. Mostly, I pretend it doesn't exist unless someone needs something, and even then, I quietly take care of it without them knowing."

She frowned. "Your brothers don't know?"

"Most of them do not. It's not unusual for club members to live in the compound and help out around the property in exchange for room and board. That's what I do. I cook. I look after the Littles. I fix things when they're broken. I run errands and fill in when someone needs me. But I also make problems go away sometimes."

She smiled. "No one would ever know."

"That's the idea. It's also why I never dated another woman after Valerie."

"Until me."

He tapped her nose. "Until you."

"You don't trust easily."

"I do not."

She rocked forward, untangled her legs, and slid her body down so she was plastered against his side. With her hand on his chest, she said, "I don't care about your money."

"I know you don't, Angel." He wrapped his arm around her, held her close, and kissed the top of her head. "If I'd had any doubts, I wouldn't have told you. I also wouldn't have claimed you."

For a long time, they lay there in silence, her stroking a finger around his chest.

Finally, he said, "I hired a private investigator to find out why Joseph is here."

She lifted her head. "When did you have time to do that?"

"After you went to sleep. I made a few calls. Joseph used his full name on the paperwork he filled out yesterday. It shouldn't be hard to find him. I expect my PI will have information this morning." He cupped the back of her neck. "Are you mad?"

She shook her head. "No. Relieved. I've been trying not to think about him or why he's here."

"No matter what his motive is, he can't get to you, Angel. I promise."

"Okay."

"I do need you to promise me you'll stay in the clubhouse at all times if I'm not with you. Don't even go outside to play."

"Okay, Daddy. I won't." She relaxed against him once more. "Thank you."

He hugged her tight. "You're mine, Little one. No thanks are necessary. I will always protect you."

After a few minutes, he rolled her to her back, rose up to lean over her, and met her gaze. "I'll go to your apartment and get whatever you want. When I get back, you can shower and get dressed. Then we'll check in with my PI, okay?"

An odd, slow smile spread across her face. "You're going to leave me in your bedroom alone?"

He chuckled. "Not a chance. I'll leave you in the kitchen with whichever Littles are here this morning. I'm sure there will be a brother around willing to keep an eye on you so you don't get up to mischief."

She rolled her pretty eyes.

"I'm pretty sure King is off rotation today. He's a firefighter, so he works three-day shifts and then has time off. There's also Rock. Have you met Rock yet?"

"Is he Atlas and Remi's father?"

"Yep. That's him."

"I've met him a few times. Is he not married?"

"No. His wife passed a long time ago. He hasn't found another Little to share his life with. Hopefully, one day, he will. In the meantime, he's always willing to help babysit."

She giggled. "Babysit. That's silly."

"Is it?" He lifted her hand to his lips and kissed her fingers.

"Seems to me like you're probably naughty enough that you can't be trusted. If I left you alone, you'd have these fingers rubbing your pussy before I made it to my bike."

Her pretty cheeks flushed. "Daddy..."

"God, I love that sound." He shoved off the bed. If he didn't get moving soon, he would end up yanking the shirt over her head and ravaging her with his mouth. He was sure she would enjoy it but didn't want to rush her. He'd pushed her pretty far last night, making her come twice, but he'd hardly needed to touch her to accomplish that. The next time she came, he wanted it to be with her naked, sprawled out for him, and begging him to suck her pussy.

CHAPTER
TWELVE

"Where's Bear?" Eden asked as she slid into the seat next to Addie at the breakfast table.

"He went to my apartment to get me some clothes." Addie took another bite of her toasted frozen waffle.

"So, no pancakes, I guess." Eden sighed dramatically.

Addie giggled. "Rock made me frozen waffles. They're good. He even has blueberry ones."

Rock headed over and handed Eden a sippy cup of milk. "But if my waffles aren't good enough for you..." he warned.

Eden sat up taller. "Waffles sound amazing, Rock. Thank you."

Rock snickered as he returned to the toaster. "I thought so."

King sat across from the two Littles, sipping a cup of coffee.

"If Bear isn't back in time, my Daddy can take us to class," Eden said.

"Oh, shoot. I forgot we have algebra this morning. I promised Bear I wouldn't leave the clubhouse for any reason. Hopefully, he'll be back by then." She finished her waffles and stood, intending to take her plate to the dishwasher, but King interrupted her and removed the plate from her hand.

"Sit," he directed.

She sighed as she returned to her chair next to Eden. "I'm not allowed to go to work either. I hope someone told Kade." She set her elbow on the table and leaned her cheek on her palm.

"Kade knows, Little one," King informed her. "He also brought your purse and backpack in from the front desk last night. He locked them up safe for you. I'll go get them."

Addie turned her forehead toward her palm and groaned. "I'm such a mess I forgot about my belongings being at the reception desk."

Eden rubbed her back. "Understandable. You had a weird evening."

Weird didn't even begin to describe all the things that had happened to Addie from the moment Joseph had walked into the shop to now. Weird was an understatement.

King returned with her stuff while Rock set a plate in front of Eden.

Addie took out her notebook. "If I can't work, I guess I should at least look over our notes in case we have a pop quiz in algebra today."

"I should look over your notes, too," Eden said between bites. "You're so much better at algebra than me."

"That's because I've taken it before, remember? This is a refresher for me."

Eden grinned. "Yep. Let's go with that. It sounds a lot better than admitting I'm not that great at math."

Addie giggled, grateful that she'd met Eden and formed a friendship. Lord knew where Addie might be today if she hadn't had Eden. She wrapped an arm around her and gave her a hug. "Thank you."

Eden hugged her back. "You're welcome. Thank you for helping me with math."

"Daddy..." Addie argued an hour later as she stood in the bathroom with her hands on her hips. "I need to shut the door while I shower."

He chuckled as he set a clean towel and a washcloth on the vanity. "Angel, this is officially the last time you'll be washing your own body. Now, you can either do so with the door open, or if you want to continue debating the topic, I'll stand in the room with you."

She barely grasped the second half of his speech because she was still focused on the first sentence. "You're going to wash me?" Her voice squeaked.

"Yep. I'm going to give you baths from now on. Starting tonight."

She swallowed. The thought of him running his hands all over her naked body made her squeeze her legs together. She was fortunate he'd provided her with a new pair of panties from the supply closet and a borrowed pair of leggings, so she hadn't had to sit at breakfast in just her T-shirt.

He cupped her face. "Or, if you'd rather, I can strip your clothes off and give you your first bath right now."

She licked her lips, considering her options. She could put up a fuss and test him.

"Angel, you might want to rethink whatever's brewing in that pretty head of yours..."

Flinching, she reconsidered. "I'll leave the door open." She was learning that arguing with him would never be in her best interest. She would not win, and he was likely to take away privileges if she kept it up.

"Good girl. Five minutes." He lifted her fingers to his lips and sucked on the middle one, making her gasp. "What's the rule?"

"I won't touch myself, Daddy."

"Not more than necessary."

"I think I'll need more than five minutes, though. I need to shave, wash my hair, and do conditioner."

"Ten minutes, and I'm going to stick my head in the door in five to make sure you're behaving." He released her and turned to walk out of the room, leaving the door open several inches.

She didn't dare touch it, nor did she risk dawdling. She quickly stripped off her clothes and stepped into the shower. She probably should have turned it on first, but it was too late for that now.

While the water heated, angled away from her, she shaved her legs. By the time she was finished with the razor, the water was hot. The glass walls were steamed up, too, so Daddy wouldn't see much when he checked on her.

She grabbed the shampoo next. Her nipples were so hard and tight, and her pussy was tingling. She knew why. It was because the banter with her Daddy about shutting the door and washing her had made her horny.

Thinking about him giving her a bath that night was going to have her squirming all day. How was she going to focus in class?

She was glad he'd gotten back soon enough that she could shower and get to class on time. She also knew he was concerned and would not only be driving her and Eden himself but also waiting outside the door to the classroom.

Addie had met Eden on the first day of class. The two of them had been the only ones who weren't eighteen-year-old freshmen, so they'd hit it off. That first day, Eden had warned Addie that she had a super overprotective boyfriend waiting for her outside and that he would also come with them when they met to study.

It had seemed so odd to Addie, odd enough that she'd been leery about this new friend of hers, and it had taken several classes before she'd met Eden at the library. She'd forced herself to do so because the truth was she hadn't made friends in town yet, and she'd really liked Eden.

It had turned out that Gabriel was a gem among gems. Sure, he'd been overprotective, but not in a creepy, jealous boyfriend way. More like a caring, I-don't-want-anything-to-happen-to-you way.

And now, the table had turned. Bear would take the two of them to class, playing the role of overprotective boyfriend. Gabriel wouldn't go with them this morning because they didn't need two bodyguards. One would suffice, and Addie's relationship with Bear was too new for him to turn her over to one of his brothers.

She smiled as she rinsed off her hair and added conditioner. She had shaved her legs, but now she picked up the razor again, deciding to shave her pussy. Could she do it? She hadn't ever done so before. Three months ago, her mother had sent her to a spa before the wedding for the "full works." It had turned out that the treatment included a Brazilian wax.

Addie had been nervous as hell when she'd spread her legs open and let a kind woman rip the hair off her private parts, but her mother had insisted Joseph would be pleased.

Ha. Joseph had never seen her pussy, and he never would. She wasn't even convinced he would have seen her naked if she'd gone through with the wedding. That's how much interest the man had shown in her.

The marriage had been arranged, so it wasn't really surprising that he'd been just as uninterested in her as she'd been in him. But as the weeks had ticked by, she'd begun to wonder if perhaps he'd had a secret girlfriend on the side and if he'd intended to continue seeing her after the wedding. It was certainly possible and apparently not uncommon among society's elite.

Addie shuddered to think she'd almost married the man. What the hell was he doing in town, though?

"Addie?"

She jumped, twisting around. She could barely make out her Daddy where he stood in the doorway. She hoped he couldn't see her any better because she had one foot propped up on the shower bench, and she'd been two seconds from dragging the razor over her private parts. If she'd already set the razor on her skin, she might have cut herself when he'd entered.

"Are you okay?" he asked.

"Yes. Fine. Can I have my other five minutes now?" she snipped.

He chuckled. "That depends. What are you about to do with that razor, Angel?"

Shit. Apparently, he could see her better than she saw him. "Shave, of course. Go away."

He stepped farther into the bathroom. "Have you shaved your pussy before, Addie?"

Well, double shit. "Do you have no boundaries at all?" she countered.

"None. Not with you. Please be careful. I don't want you to nick your skin. Then you'd end up in Doc's office with your legs spread while he examined the cuts."

She sighed and set her foot back on the floor. "I assumed you'd like me shaved down there," she murmured, "but now I'm shaking too badly to do it."

"Addie, you may keep your pussy however you prefer. Shaved, groomed, a landing strip, not cut at all… I don't care. Do it for *you*, not for *me*, okay?"

Why did he have to be so sweet and overbearing at the same time? His kindness diluted his gruff exterior and left her reeling. "Okay," she whispered. Now, she wondered what she might prefer. She'd never thought about it. She'd only been thinking of him.

Instead of leaving her with her own embarrassment, he continued, "I assume at some point you were shaved or waxed bare in the past, based on the growth, Angel. Did you make that decision for yourself?"

What was he, psychic? How had he figured that out from the minimal contact he'd had with her pussy without looking last night? "No," she muttered as she moved to stand directly under the warm spray. It was so weird having this conversation with him while she stood in his shower and he watched fully clothed from a few feet away. Even though the steam would be making it difficult for him to make out specifics, she was still naked.

"Then how about we discuss this topic later before you make a decision? If you like the feeling of having your pussy bare, I'll shave it for you, okay?"

The water was perfectly warm, bordering on hot, but she shivered anyway. "Can I please have my other five minutes, Daddy?"

"Yes, Angel." He finally turned and left the room.

Addie stood under the spray for the entire five minutes, letting it run down her hair to rinse off the conditioner. He kept doing this to her, pushing her to discuss topics that regular people probably never talked about, embarrassing her to the point that her face was always hot and red.

She should put her foot down and be more forceful about her boundaries. Except Bear had made it clear she would have no boundaries with him. On top of that, his intimate discussions about such private matters made her horny every time. He knew it; that's why he did it.

"Are you ready to get out, Angel?" He was back. Not surprising. She'd used up far more than her allotted time.

"Yes, Sir." She turned off the water and didn't even care that he opened the shower door, held out a huge towel, and wrapped her up in it.

She didn't care when he guided her to the middle of the bathroom and patted her body dry. She also didn't care when he removed the towel and used it to wring out her hair.

If she were honest with herself, she'd probably stayed in the shower too long on purpose. She'd kind of wanted him to see her naked. The entire time he fussed over her, making sure every drop of water was absorbed, she watched him in the bathroom mirror.

What she saw in his expression was lust and admiration. That's all that mattered. After being engaged to a man who had never glanced at her, she found it refreshing to date a man who couldn't take his eyes off her.

"Thank you, Daddy," she said as he hung the towel up and grabbed a comb.

"You're welcome, Angel." He didn't make a single comment about the fact that she stood naked in his bathroom while he grabbed a comb and carefully worked out the tangles in her long hair.

By the time he was done, she no longer cared either. After all, he was her Daddy. He'd been destined to see her naked. He'd promised her he wouldn't wait long. She might as well get over herself because the fluttering feeling in her belly made every moment of his care worth it.

CHAPTER
THIRTEEN

"How was class?" Bear asked as soon as Addie and Eden were buckled in the SUV.

"Good," Addie said.

Eden grumbled next to her. "That's because you're a math whiz. I'm pretty sure I flunked that quiz."

Addie turned toward her friend. "We can study together more often now. You'll get it."

"Thank you. I appreciate your help. Math is not my friend."

Addie was grateful for the distraction of the class and for having someone to talk to. It kept her mind off the fact that Joseph would be coming in to talk to Kade about his "bike" later that afternoon. *As if he has any interest in bikes...*

As soon as they pulled into the compound, Addie said, "I should get to the desk. I feel bad about abandoning Kade all morning."

Bear stopped her before she could skip away. He wrapped an arm around her middle and hauled her in close. "Slow down, Angel. Lunch first, and then we'll see what's happening at the bike shop. You're not going there alone, remember?" He lifted a brow.

"Yes, Sir." She sighed. No sense arguing with him.

Gabriel was in the kitchen when they entered, and he immediately sent both Littles to put their backpacks in their apartments and wash their hands. Five minutes later, they were sitting at the table eating grilled cheese sandwiches cut into triangles and tomato soup.

"I'm getting spoiled here," Addie said as she dug into her food.

Bear sat next to her with twice as much food in front of him. "That's the idea. It's how we keep our girlfriends around. Lure them in with food so they never want to leave."

Eden giggled. "And spankings. Don't forget spankings."

Addie grinned. "I'm not sure I would stay just for the spankings. But the pancakes, sandwiches, and chicken nuggets have given me something to think about."

Bear nudged her in the ribs before leaning in to whisper in her ear, "I'll give you a few more things to think about as soon as you're ready."

Her cheeks heated as she dipped her sandwich in the soup and took another bite. It was a struggle not to squirm.

Eden set her spoon down and said, "You didn't get a chance to try Bear's hot chocolate last night. We managed to get in trouble before the popcorn and hot chocolate."

Bear chuckled. "We'll try again soon."

When they were done, Addie said, "I really should get to the desk, Daddy. Kade is going to fire me."

He took her hand and led her the other direction, toward the wing with the apartments. "Trust me, Kade is not going to fire you. Your job is safe."

She tugged on his hand. "We're going in the wrong direction." If they went back to his apartment, they would end up kissing, and probably more, and she would never get to work.

"I want to talk to you about something first, Little one." They reached his door, and he let them in before leading her to the sofa. "Sit."

She sat next to him, worried now because he was so seri-ous. "What's wrong?"

"Nothing. I just wanted to tell you that I spoke to my PI while you were in class and to tell you what I found out."

"Oh." She sat straighter as Daddy took her hand in his.

"My guy isn't done digging. He hasn't had enough time to gather much information yet, but he did figure out that your ex is staying at the hotel on the edge of town. He also bought that bike from a junkyard, so you're right that his story about the bike belonging to his father is fake. The question is, why is he here? I don't like it."

She frowned. "I don't understand either. Do you think he knows I work here, then?"

"Definitely. He's a wealthy guy. I'm sure he has his own private investigator who easily found you. I'd bet he knows the address of your apartment, your class schedule, and your job information."

She shuddered. "Why?"

"We're going to find that out. Now, here's the question. Do you want to face him yourself when he comes in this after-noon? Or would you rather let me handle it?"

She shook her head. "I'll talk to him. I can't imagine he means me any harm. If he thinks he can talk me into coming back home and marrying him, I need to be firm and tell him it's never happening."

"That's for damn sure, Angel, but I can handle that for you."

"No. I should do it myself. I should've done it a long time ago. It was cowardly of me to run off right before the cere-mony. I should've faced him and broken it off long before that."

Bear reached up and tucked a lock of hair behind her ear. "You are my brave girl. You can't beat yourself up over the past. You were under a lot of pressure. I'm proud of you for figuring out you were making a mistake before you walked down that aisle. Damn glad, too. I will allow you to talk to him, but not alone, understood?"

She drew in a slow breath and held his gaze. "Maybe it would be better if I met him somewhere for coffee or something."

Daddy shook his head. "I don't like it, Angel. I'd rather you spoke with him here at the compound."

She lowered her gaze, thinking.

Bear lifted her chin. "I know it happened fast, Addie, but you're my life. I can't in good conscience let you do something that might be dangerous. Meeting up with your ex after he came into the shop under false pretenses doesn't make me feel warm and fuzzy. Meeting up with him alone somewhere public makes me even more nervous. Can you understand how I feel?"

She nodded. What if Bear's ex, Valerie, showed up in town and asked Bear to meet her for drinks, and he took off and left Addie stewing? She'd be livid. "You're right."

He grabbed the back of her neck and pulled her in for a quick kiss that made her toes curl.

Kade stuck his head into the reception area an hour later. "He's on his way. Said he'd be here in five minutes."

Addie's hands shook as she straightened the folders in front of her for the millionth time. She wasn't a very good employee today. She was far too worried and distracted to focus, and that added to her stress. She needed to apologize to Kade for her horrible work ethic today. He wasn't paying her to bring her ex-fiancé drama into his shop.

"You okay?" Bear asked as soon as Kade ducked back out. He was sitting on a tall stool next to her behind the desk.

"Not really," she admitted.

He jumped down from the stool, grabbed the back of her jeans, and tugged so she had to stumble backward against him. As soon as his arms came around her and his lips landed on her ear, she calmed. "I'll be right here the entire time. I won't let anything happen to you. If he's not polite, I'll ask him to leave. If you get uncomfortable, you walk right out the door behind us."

"Okay." She liked the way he distracted her with his huge hand on her tummy, his thumb grazing the underside of her breast. Maybe it was ridiculous that she could be tempted by him while she was under this much stress, but she appreciated it anyway.

Two minutes later, Bear was back on the stool, and Addie watched out the front windows as Joseph strolled toward the office and stepped inside.

His eyes widened as if he was surprised to see her. "Adelaine." He rubbed his hands together as he approached the counter.

She bristled at the use of her full name. Not a single person from her old life, including Joseph, had ever honored her preference for Addie. "What are you doing here, Joseph?"

"You don't look surprised to see me."

"Nope. I was here when you came in yesterday. I just didn't show myself. I know your father never owned a bike, so what are you doing in town?"

He sighed. "I wanted to talk to you. Can we go somewhere private?" He glanced at Bear.

Addie didn't need to look over her shoulder to know that Bear was probably shooting daggers at him with his eyes. He didn't interrupt, though. Bless him. He'd said he would let her handle this up until it got out of control, and he was honoring his word. "No. You can talk to me right here."

Joseph nodded toward Bear without looking at him again.

"You don't need a bodyguard, Adelaine. I'm not going to hurt you."

"Addie."

"What?" His brows furrowed.

"I hate the name Adelaine. I go by Addie. I told you that when we met, and several other times, but you didn't listen."

He winced slightly. "I'm sorry. Your mother—"

Addie's heart rate sped up at the mention of her mother. She planted her hands on the counter and leaned forward. "My mother is single. Why don't you marry her if you're going to follow her orders like a dog."

Behind her, Bear's breath hitched. Addie was pretty sure he chuckled.

Joseph's eyes widened. "You're right."

"Thank you. Now, what are you doing here?"

"I was hoping to talk some sense into you."

Addie stiffened. "Pardon?"

He sighed. "Please, Adel…Addie. Just talk to me. We make sense, you and I. I know I didn't handle things well. I should've spent more time with you, but I see that now. I'm sorry. I'm here to apologize. I want you to consider coming home with me. We can build something meaningful."

She scrunched up her face. "We make sense? Do you know how ridiculous that sounds?"

He winced again and ran a hand over his head. He glanced at Bear again. "Could we please talk alone somewhere?"

"No." She shook her head and crossed her arms in front of her. "It's here or nowhere."

Joseph turned to face Bear. "Do you mind? She doesn't need some giant biker bouncer protecting her from me. If you're worried about her safety, at least step out front so we can have some privacy."

Addie was actually impressed by Joseph's suggestion, but she knew Bear would never go for it.

"Not a chance," Bear growled, his first words since Joseph

had entered. "Speak your peace and go." At least he didn't move from his perch on the stool.

Addie didn't look over her shoulder at Bear. She knew if she did, she would lose her composure. She may have been a weakling for the past five years, but she was done with that life. She was stronger now. She loved that she had a man she could count on who would take her in his arms and soothe her while she fell apart after this confrontation was over, but she wanted Joseph to see a strong, independent woman. Even though she had a Little inside her, who adored the pampering that came with having a Daddy, she wasn't that girl who'd let everyone trample over her. Not anymore. Joseph needed to know it.

Joseph sighed dramatically before turning his attention back to Addie. "Adelaine. Addie. Think about this. Our families are equal members of society. Uniting them will make both of our families more powerful. It's a logical union."

Addie stared at him. Was he insane? "Why would two people get married just to make their families more powerful? This is the twenty-first century. Who does that?"

"Lots of people do. Don't be naïve, Addie."

"Don't be condescending, Joseph," she shot back. "I'm not marrying you. End of story. I'm sorry I didn't come to my senses sooner, but I'm glad I realized what a mistake I was making before I walked down that aisle—and you know it, too. You can't possibly have feelings for me. We hardly spoke before the ceremony. This is the longest conversation I've had with you, cumulatively, the entire time I've known you. Plus, you've never once looked me in the eye before. I wasn't even a human being to you. I was just some girl your parents told you to marry."

He cringed. Good. "And I'm sorry for that. I realize my fault in all this. I want to try again. I can be better. I can do better. I promise. Give me a chance. What are you doing working here at this used bike repair shop for a gang, Adelaine?"

So much for remembering her name.

Bear growled. "Watch it, asshole. This is a motorcycle club. Not a gang. And every member of this club is a bigger man than you."

Joseph ignored him, which was impressive considering that it was almost certain Bear had his hands fisted and his face contorted in a menacing way. Bear could take Joseph out with one swing—he wouldn't even need to. He could pick the man up by the shirt collar and toss him out on the street without breaking a sweat or taking a single swing.

The thought made Addie fight a giggle. In fact, she had to cover her mouth because she was grinning like a loon.

"What's so funny?" Joseph grumbled.

She swallowed and straightened. "Nothing. Look, we're not getting back together. It's not happening."

His nostrils flared. She hadn't thought him capable of that level of emotion. "Addie… Honey."

She blinked.

Bear growled again.

Joseph cleared his throat. "You can't hide here in this dinky town forever. Your mother will cut you off completely if you don't come back with me."

"Ohhh. So, you did plot with my mother."

"Don't twist this around, Addie." His frustration was growing. Good. "Of course, I spoke with her. So did my parents."

Addie rolled her eyes. "Nothing has changed. You all met to discuss my life as though any of you have any say in my decisions. I don't care if my mother cuts me off, Joseph. In fact, I'll be relieved. It's tidier. I don't need servants, designer clothes, fancy jewelry, expensive cars, manicures, spa treatments, steak restaurants, and a country club membership. I don't even want those things."

"So, your plan is to waste away in that dingy apartment in this stupid nowhere town, working for a gang of bikers for the rest of your life?"

"Yep. Sounds like heaven to me. These people treat me with respect. They talk to me as though my opinion matters. They look me in the eyes. They do nice things for me. That's worth more than all the money in the world. You can tell my mother I don't want her money."

"You're her only heir, Adelaine," he shouted, throwing his hands up.

Addie chuckled. "Then she should take some nice vacations and leave her wealth to a homeless shelter or bury it with her. I don't care what she does with it. I'm not coming home. Case closed."

She was pretty proud of herself. Addie had never in her life been so confrontational with another person. She hadn't been sure she'd had it in her. Apparently, she had more of a spine than she'd thought.

"I think it's time for you to go, Joseph," Bear growled. "You heard the lady. She's not interested in what you're selling."

Joseph shot a glare at Bear. "Stay out of it."

Addie didn't need to look over her shoulder. She felt Bear's presence as he rose from the stool and stepped behind her. She didn't mind if he staked his claim on her in front of Joseph, but she thought she would appear more independent and firm if she didn't use Bear as a reason she wasn't going home.

Sure, she was falling head over heels in love with the giant, growly man at her back, but meeting him and becoming his woman had nothing to do with the fact that she would never return to her former life. He was the icing on the cake.

She could feel Bear's heat, but he didn't touch her. He just imposed his huge presence behind her.

"You should go, Joseph. We're not getting back together. We were never together in the first place. You have no feelings for me. You're just being a lap dog for your parents. It's not attractive. Why don't you find someone you actually love and then get married? It's not going to be me. Your life will be so much more fulfilling if you marry someone you choose instead of letting your parents do it for you."

Joseph stared at her for a long time as if she had two heads. "I'm not leaving without you, Adelaine." He'd given up honoring her request entirely. "I'll go for now. I'll give you some time to think about what a colossal mistake you're making. When I speak to your mother tonight, I'll tell her we're working things out. I won't tell her about this shitty job you have or the rundown apartment you're living in. You think about how much better your life would be with me, and we'll talk again."

She opened her mouth to tell him not to bother, but he spun around so fast and walked out the door that she didn't get the chance.

Bear's hands were on her shoulders before the door fully closed. "Do you have any idea how fucking hot I am for you right now?"

CHAPTER
FOURTEEN

t had taken every ounce of self-control for Bear to perch behind Addie and let her handle her ex by herself. What he'd wanted to do was wrap her in his arms and tell that rich boy to take a hike because Addie was Bear's girl.

He hadn't done it, though, and he was glad because Addie had needed to voice all of that and get it out of her system. He hadn't wanted to interrupt and inform Joseph that he'd missed his opportunity because it was better for Addie if Joseph didn't know that another, better man had filled the shoes he could not.

Addie had been so fucking amazing. Gorgeous. She hadn't faltered for a moment, and he was so proud of her.

Now that Joseph was gone, however, Bear slid his arms around her middle and kissed her neck. "You were spectacular, Angel," he whispered in her ear. "I'm so proud of you."

She slumped against him, trembling now that it was over.

Bear grabbed the water bottle from the desk, twisted off the top, and handed it to her. "Take a drink, Addie."

Her hand was shaking so badly that he had to help her steady the bottle, but she managed to take several sips. "I can't believe I did that." She spun around, beaming. "I've never stood up for myself like that before. I didn't even know I could."

He rubbed her shoulders. "You did, and you shocked him."

She shrugged. "I didn't know that I could shock him. He doesn't know me at all."

"Why on Earth do you suppose he wants you to marry him?" Something felt off about the entire thing. There was something Joseph had not said. "Do you think someone is holding something over him? Maybe he can't access his inheritance or something if he doesn't marry you...?"

Addie shrugged. "I don't know. It makes no sense. Mine isn't the only family that would be a good merger for him. I think my mother worked pretty hard to choose Joseph for me. She was ecstatic about uniting our families. I was so numb to the situation that I didn't think hard about it. For the last year, I spent most of my time losing sleep, pacing, vomiting, and all but pulling my hair out. My focus was only on my fate. I didn't stop to ponder why she insisted on Joseph. It was just my life. The life she wanted me to live. I was weak and—"

Bear pressed two fingers to her lips. "Stop berating yourself, Angel. You were young and under a lot of pressure. You took a huge risk, and it was very brave of you to walk away. Not many twenty-two-year-old women would have the guts to cut ties with their families for any reason. In your case, the financial hit was huge."

She took a deep breath. "I guess. I still feel foolish for letting it get that far. It's like I snapped that day. Like I'd been in a trance and someone said the magic words, and I suddenly had clarity. There was no way I could go through with that farce. I thought of nothing else but running as far and fast as I could. I've never looked back. I'm not sorry. Even before I met you, I knew I made the right decision. I don't care if I have to work three jobs and eat boxed mac and cheese for a few years to finish the college degree I want if it means making my own choices and getting out from under my mother's thumb."

He pulled her closer, splaying his hands on her back. "Well, you don't have to work *any* jobs if you don't want to, and I'm only feeding you that boxed macaroni with powdered cheese on the nights the Littles stage a mutiny. Some of them love that shit."

She giggled. "Sometimes, I crave it."

He made a disgusted face, pretending to puke. "You're not alone. It must be a Little-girl trait."

She wrapped her arms tightly around him and hugged as hard as she could, and damn, but it felt so right. For years, he'd been living a bit of a lie, always watching everyone else find love and happiness while insisting he didn't want that for himself. Now, love had dropped right in his lap, and he was so fucking thankful.

After a long hug that calmed both their hearts, he leaned her back. "You don't have to worry about finances, Addie. You realize that, right?"

She shrugged. "I want to do this on my own. I want to get a finance degree, and I want to feel like I earned it. I don't want someone else to pay for it. Not my mother, and not you. Do you understand that?"

He didn't like it, but he understood. "Yes, Angel. I get it." His chest was tight from being so damn proud of her. "Will you let me cover everything else? I bet it would lift a lot of pressure off you if you didn't have rent and utilities on top of tuition. What if your wages went to tuition, and you let me handle the rest?"

"You can't pay my rent, Bear."

He lifted a brow. "There won't be any rent, Addie. You don't need your apartment anymore. You're certainly not paying rent to move into my apartment."

"Oh."

He chuckled. "Did you forget you live with me now?"

She shrugged. "Yeah. Sort of. It's been like a day. I'm still wrapping my head around it. You really want me to move in with you?"

"Absolutely."

"What if you change your mind or we aren't as compatible after we get to know each other? I should probably keep my apartment for a while in case you get tired of me."

He narrowed his gaze, grinning. "Angel, I am never going to tire of you. Not in a million-billion years. You're mine." He slid a hand around to her chest and flattened it between her breasts. "Can you feel it in here, Little one?"

Her eyes were wide, but she nodded. "Yeah, but I don't trust it yet, Daddy. It's foreign."

"That's fair. I'll give you until the end of the week to realize I'm right," he teased.

"Ha ha."

"You won't need that long," he told her, all cocky.

The door to the shop opened, and Kade stepped in. "How'd it go?"

Bear let Addie turn around in his arms to face Kade.

"Weird," Addie told him.

"Should I pretend to look over that hunk of junk he brought in for me to fix?" he joked.

She shook her head. "No. Daddy said Joseph bought it from a junkyard."

Kade laughed. "He told me. Don't worry. I already put it in the truck to return it to the junkyard. Do you think he's coming back?"

Bear growled. "Unfortunately, yes."

Kade sobered, his brows furrowing. "I'll make sure the guys keep an eye out for him."

Bear nodded. "I'm not leaving Addie alone in this office, so I'll be in here whenever she is for now."

Kade nodded. "Addie, you don't have to continue working for me, Little one. I know your circumstances have changed."

She shook her head as Bear knew she would. "I want to.

I'm sorry I've made such a mess of things lately, but if you'll give me another chance, I promise I'll be a good employee."

Kade took another step closer. "Addie, Little one, you haven't made a mess of anything. Nothing that happened is your fault. You're the best receptionist I've had in a long time. Most people I hire don't really want to do the job, and nothing gets done."

"It's not a difficult job. They'd have to be really lazy to be that inept," she murmured.

Kade chuckled. "There are a lot of lazy people out there."

"Well, even though I didn't have any references, and I've never been anyone's receptionist before, I appreciate you taking a chance on me. I can do it." She stood taller.

"I have no doubt you can, Addie," Kade agreed. "I just want you to know that I'll understand if you talk things over with Bear and change your mind at any point. I'll still think the world of you. You're a member of my family now, Little one."

Bear nearly choked up at Kade's speech. It felt really good knowing his brothers had his Little girl's back. He'd never doubted they would, but now that it was truly his turn, and he needed their careful observation and help to keep her safe, he was humbled to have everyone rallying behind him.

"Thank you, Kade," Addie said softly. "It's been a long time since I've had family I could count on. Not even blood family. You all are the best." She wiped a tear from her cheek.

Bear kissed the top of her head.

Kade smiled warmly. "Why don't you take the rest of the afternoon off? You've had a stressful day."

She shook her head vehemently. "No, thank you. I'd rather be busy."

"Okay, Little one, but if you change your mind, just go on inside. We'll manage. Lord knows we've had to in the past."

"Thank you."

Bear smiled at his brother over Addie's head. "Yes, Kade. Thank you."

"Anytime." Kade turned and headed back into the shop.

"You okay, Angel?" Bear asked as he turned her around to face him.

"No, but I will be. I just need time to process all of this. It's a lot. Even without Joseph showing up, it's a lot to take in."

"I understand. I'll be right here with you. How about I let you do your thing while I call and check in with the PI?"

"Okay." She hugged him tightly yet again.

He could feel her need for comfort, and he wished she would let him carry her to their apartment so he could tuck her in for a nap, but she would balk at that idea. She was still feeling the high from confronting her ex. He needed to let her ride that.

In a few hours, she was going to crash, and he would be there to catch her and take care of her. He would always be there to catch her.

CHAPTER
FIFTEEN

"You meant it, huh? You really take this Daddying job seriously." Addie stood next to the vanity in their bathroom, watching as her Daddy filled the tub with water. He'd even added toys and bubbles.

"Yep." He turned toward her. "When we're in the clubhouse, especially in our apartment, you don't have to make decisions. I'll take care of you."

"That sounds both scary and exciting. I can't remember when anyone last took care of me. I guess my parents did when I was a baby, but no one has in a long time."

He smoothed his hands down her arms. "I'm here now."

"Aren't you exhausted from dealing with all my shit? Wouldn't you rather drop into bed and leave me to my own defenses? I can take a bath without help, you know."

She watched his face as his chest heaved with his chuckle. "Angel, I literally draw energy from caring for you. It's like fuel to me."

She leaned into him hard and wrapped her arms around him. He was quickly becoming her whole world. It was scary and such a relief at the same time. Could this really last? It felt so real, so genuine, so right.

"Let's get you in the tub," he murmured, his voice gravelly, likely due to the same emotions she felt.

She didn't say a word as he pulled her shirt over her head and dropped it in the clothes hamper. She grabbed his shoulders as he removed her shoes, socks, jeans, and, finally, her panties and bra.

A shudder wracked her body as his palms slid up from her thighs to her waist. "You're so gorgeous, Addie," he whispered in that same sexy voice. "Do you want me to wash your hair or pin it up?"

"I washed it this morning."

He opened a drawer and grabbed a scrunchy.

Her eyes widened when she saw how many hair bobbles he had in that drawer. Most of them had tags on them or were still in their packaging. He'd filled that for her. Probably today. When had he had time?

She tipped her head forward to let him pull her long hair up in a bun on top of her head. When he was done, he rose and lifted her off the floor to set her in the tub. "On your bottom, Angel."

As he poured bubbles into the stream of water, she let herself slide into a deeper Little space.

Daddy was in his element. He obviously took this role very seriously. It was important to him. He wasn't taking care of her because he felt obligated. He was doing so because it was in his DNA.

When he handed her a Barbie, she gasped and held it above the water. "She'll get wet, Daddy."

He chuckled. "She's a bathtime Barbie. She's meant to get wet."

Addie frowned as she thought about messing up her doll's hair. Sudden emotions came out of nowhere, making Addie choke up as her hands started shaking.

"Hey there, Little one. What's wrong?" He cupped her chin

and tipped her head back. His brow was deeply furrowed as he searched her gaze.

"I just realized something I haven't thought about in years."

"What's that, Angel?"

"My mother didn't let me play with my toys."

His eyes widened.

Addie swallowed. "She wanted my room to always look perfect. It was like a child's dream in a display home. When she wasn't around, my father would take things down and let me play with them, and then he'd put them back so she wouldn't know. It was like our silent secret. It wasn't worth arguing with her. He knew it, too. I never thought about it until just now."

She trembled as she continued to hold the Barbie out of the water.

Daddy looked emotional, too. He swallowed hard, and his eyes were watery. "I'm so sorry. Let's make new memories. Dunk that Barbie in the water. She's meant to be played with. She's even wearing a bathing suit."

Addie stared at the doll and murmured to herself, "I could even take it off if I wanted to."

"Of course."

"Does she have other clothes?"

"Sure. And if there's something you want her to wear, we'll buy it. Soon, her tiny shoes and accessories will be all over the apartment," he teased.

Tears welled up in her eyes. "Is this why I'm attracted to the idea of being Little? Because I didn't get to be a child much when I was young?"

"Could be. It happens sometimes. There are a lot of reasons why someone enjoys age play. It might be because they didn't have toys growing up or because they had everything and loved that stage of life. And anything in between. I've seen

Littles get emotional over a box of crayons because they never had a new box growing up, for example."

She stared at him. "I had plenty of crayons, but I wasn't allowed to use them and mess up the box."

He winced. "I'm so sorry. From now on, you'll use your crayons and markers. Play with your toys. Make messes. I won't even complain if I step on a Barbie shoe," he teased.

She wiped away the tears and giggled. "You'd crush it, Daddy. You're so big."

"Probably." He pointed at the Barbie. "Take the plunge, Little one. Dip her in the water."

She lowered the Barbie under the water, loving the way her hair fanned out around her. Giggles erupted, and when she glanced at Bear, he was smiling.

"Good girl. You play while I wash you."

She tried to focus on the doll while Bear grabbed a washcloth and poured liquid soap on it. He started with her back, gently stroking over her skin before moving to her arms, which caused her to have to shift the Barbie back and forth from one hand to the other.

Addie found herself surprisingly comfortable even though she was completely naked and he was fully dressed. She dipped the doll in and out of the water, running her fingers over the soft, fake hair while Daddy washed her legs and then her tummy.

When he smoothed the cloth over her breasts, her breath hitched. Her nipples hardened, yanking her into a more adult space. But when he dragged the cloth between her legs, she dropped the Barbie entirely, letting her float away.

Addie's eyes slid closed. A soft moan escaped. "Daddy…" She parted her thighs wider, grateful when he released the washcloth and used his fingers instead.

Grabbing the sides of the tub, she tipped her head back, mouth falling open. Her body fell under his spell. All inhibitions fled the room. She'd never wanted anything so badly in her life.

Daddy braced a hand on her lower back while his other stroked through her folds. "Damn, you are sexy, Addie. You bring me to my knees." He found her clit and circled it. "Can I push my finger inside you, Angel?"

She nodded. "Please." She wanted to feel him inside her. She wanted more.

Her breath hitched as he eased his middle finger into her tight channel. She'd used that vibrator inside her many times in the past few weeks, but for some reason, it felt much nicer having her Daddy stroke her instead. It was personal, and he curled that finger on his way back out, making her lift her butt off the bottom of the tub.

"That's my girl. Let it feel good," he praised.

She braced herself, white-knuckling the sides of the tub. "Daddy…" He'd touched her before, but not like this. Her legs trembled, and she fought the urge to close them over his wrist because she didn't want him to stop.

When he added another finger, she gasped. "Oh, God."

"Fuck, Addie. You're so fucking sexy. Let it go. Come on my fingers, Angel."

After thrusting into her a few more times, he reached as deep as he could and ground his palm against her clit. That was all it took. Addie cried out as a powerful orgasm claimed her.

"That's it. Milk my fingers, Addie. Damn, you're perfect."

She was panting when he finally eased his hand away from her pussy. Her body was so limp that she probably would have slipped into the water and drowned if he hadn't been holding her up.

Daddy grabbed her hips, lifted her out of the water, and stood her on her feet.

Trembling and uncertain about the ability of her legs to

hold her up, she was relieved when he quickly wrapped a towel around her and lifted her into his arms.

He carried her into the bedroom and lowered her onto her back on the bed before opening the towel and patting the rest of her dry with the corners.

Her vision was still blurry as he lowered his lips to her tummy and kissed a path up to her breast. As he captured her nipple and sucked, she grabbed his head and whimpered. "Oh, God."

He moaned against her breast, the vibrations driving her arousal back to where it had been before he'd made her come. As if he couldn't get enough, he switched breasts, treating the other one to the same attention.

She arched her chest toward his mouth, aching for him. "I want you," she whispered as she slid her hands to his shoulders. "Please, Bear, make love to me."

He released her nipple with a pop and stared down at her. "Are you sure, Angel? I don't want to rush you."

She nodded. "Positive. I've never wanted anything more." Earlier, she'd been a bit scared about what it would be like to have him inside her, but her doubts fled the room as she stared into his eyes. She wanted this man, her Daddy. She wanted him to claim her in every way. He was it for her. She knew it with a clarity she'd never felt before. "Please…"

Bear rose to standing, staring down at her as he pulled his shirt over his head. He took his time removing the rest of his clothes, revealing his amazing body fully for the first time. Every bit of him was huge. His height, his broad shoulders, his amazing pecs, abs, and biceps, but when she first set her gaze on his erection, she stopped breathing.

Don't panic. She licked her lips. "That's…" She didn't know what to say.

He leaned over the nightstand, tugged open the drawer, and snagged a foil packet. With his gaze on her, he tore it open with his teeth before rolling the condom down his length.

"Daddy…"

He slid his hands under her shoulders and hauled her to the center of the bed as he climbed up to kneel between her legs. "It will be very tight, Angel, and it might hurt for a minute the first time, but I promise, after that, it will feel so good you'll forget the pain."

She fisted the sheets at her sides, doubting him. "Okay. So, you're going to just, uh…" She couldn't control her breathing.

"No, Angel. First, I'm going to eat your precious pussy until you scream. Then, when you're sated and limp, I will ease into you. You can stop me at any time, Addie. We'll go as slow as you need or not do it at all tonight if you're not ready."

She nodded. "Okay." She wanted this. She wanted it with him. But now, all she could focus on was the first thing he'd said. *He's going to put his mouth on me…*

Spreading her thighs wide, Bear lowered his mouth and dragged his tongue slowly through her folds and over her clit.

Her eyes rolled back. *Oh. My. God.* She'd never felt anything like that. She'd never *imagined* anything like that. And he did it again. On the third pass, he thrust his tongue inside her.

Addie stopped breathing as she was bombarded with sensations. He moaned against her labia as if he were a starving man devouring his last meal. When he sucked her clit and flicked it with his tongue, she came so fast and so hard that she nearly shot off the bed. The only things tethering her to the mattress were his hands on her thighs.

She was marginally aware of him wiping his mouth on the sheets as he climbed up her body, and then his lips were on hers, kissing her with urgency.

He tasted of her, and it was heady. As he thrust his tongue into her mouth, he eased his erection into her channel.

She grabbed his hips, her fingertips digging into his firm butt cheeks. Bracing herself, she broke the kiss to gasp for oxygen. "Bear…"

He cupped her face. "Look at me, Angel. Take a deep breath."

She knew only the very tip of him was inside her, but she was nervous. Licking her lips, she met his gaze. "I'm okay."

"You sure?"

She nodded. "More please." She wanted him to fill her. She wanted to feel him deep inside her. That didn't mean she wasn't scared.

Daddy eased out and then back in slightly more.

She bucked her hips upward, forcing him deeper.

He groaned, and she was pretty sure his eyes rolled back slightly. Knowing she affected him like that was powerful and fueled her need for more. She slid her hands around to grip his butt cheeks. "Do it."

His elbows held him above her, and his arms were trembling.

"Please, Bear." She lifted her hips higher. "I need you to fill me. Stop teasing."

He hesitated a moment before thrusting all the way home.

Addie winced. The pressure was intense. He was even bigger than she'd thought, and it was so tight. The temporary pain subsided in seconds, though, leaving her with nothing but the throbbing need for friction. "Do it again," she begged.

He gave a slight chuckle. "Hang on, Angel. If I move, I'm going to come, and I don't want to—not yet. You're squeezing my cock like a vice grip. I'm two seconds from erupting."

That thought made her feel even more powerful. She'd never considered how much he would be affected by her. She squirmed while she waited, desperation consuming her. The small amount of friction he'd given her had been enough to show her how delicious it would be.

Breathing heavily, he set his forehead against hers, closed his eyes, and pulled almost all the way out before easing back in.

Addie's breath hitched. She'd had no reason to be so

concerned about sex. She'd already forgotten the wince of pain. It had been replaced with this blissful pleasure. "More."

He groaned as he gave her more, easing in and out too slowly for her taste. "Harder," she demanded.

Daddy took her mouth again, kissing the sense out of her, perhaps to get her to shut up. She didn't mind. She liked his kisses. She could easily lay in bed all day kissing Bear.

Giving her what she wanted, he grabbed her shoulders, bracing her, and thrust harder and deeper. Good thing he'd braced her, or she might have shot into the headboard.

"Addie…" Her name was reverent from his lips. A second later, he slid one hand between them, found her clit, and rubbed it.

Her need grew. She wanted everything, and he was giving it to her.

"Come for me, Angel."

For a moment, she thought he was surely kidding. How could she orgasm simply because he ordered it? But her clit seemed to swell to double its size, and her body obeyed him.

Nothing could have prepared her for how intense it would feel to orgasm around his huge erection. It was nothing like the vibrator she'd used. The impersonal plastic and rubber didn't hold a candle to the man grinding the base of his erection against her sensitive nub.

As her body pulsed around him, he continued to move, causing her orgasm to go on and on while he thrust. Every time he ground against her clit, she cried out again. The swollen nerves were too sensitive, and yet she wanted more.

With a deep groan, Bear thrust as deep as he could one last time and came. His shaft pulsed in her channel as his body jerked from the release.

Finally, he lowered most of his weight over her, dropping his forehead to the bed next to her ear.

It felt so good being covered by him with his erection still inside her. She rubbed her hands up and down his back and butt, wishing he never had to move. She'd never felt this close to another human being and hated breaking the spell.

"Angel…" The one word said so much as he breathed it into her ear, and he was still panting when he lifted some of his weight off her to look down at her face. He brushed hair from her cheek. "Are you okay?" His brow furrowed with concern.

She shook her head. "I think I died, and I'm good with that. Please don't get up yet." She gripped his butt cheeks.

He kissed all over her face before lingering for a long, slow taste of her lips. "Do you have any idea how much you mean to me, Addie?"

"Yes." She truly did because she felt the same about him.

"I'm twice your age, and I've been roaming around pretending I didn't need a Little girl in my life. And then you showed up…"

She smiled as she danced her fingers up and down his back. "I'm so glad I applied for that job."

"Me, too, Angel. Me, too. Can I pull out yet?"

"No." She shook her head. "Never."

He chuckled. "You'll need a drink soon and, eventually, food. I can probably reach my phone on the nightstand if you want me to call Gabriel to bring us something."

She giggled. "No way, Daddy."

"Are you worried he would see my ass?" he teased.

She giggled harder.

When he eased out of her, she sighed. "When can we do that again?"

He bent over and kissed her, grinning. "I just told you I'm old. Give me a few minutes to recuperate."

"You're not *that* old, Daddy." She started to lift up, but he set a hand on her chest and stopped her.

"Stay still. I'm going to get a washcloth and clean you up."

"Okay." She wasn't going to argue. He'd proven time and again that he liked taking care of her. She would let him because it was so damn sweet and made her feel like a princess.

He walked back into the room, still fully naked. The condom was gone, but his erection was still just as huge as it had been before. She stared at it while he spread her thighs wider and gently cleaned her skin.

"Does it meet your satisfaction?" he teased.

She didn't even hide her appraisal. Continuing to stare at his bobbing shaft, she licked her lips. "I'm not sure yet. I'll need to taste it first." She had no idea where this boldness came from, but she found herself seriously wanting to explore his body.

His breath hitched, and he tossed the washcloth on the floor before crawling over her on his hands and knees. Was it growing bigger?

When he stopped moving, his knees were near her breasts, and his shaft hovered a few inches from her mouth.

She reached with both hands to touch it. "So soft and hard at the same time."

He took deep breaths and let them out slowly.

She lifted her head and licked a line up the length, loving the moan that escaped his lips. Emboldened, she did it again before wrapping her hand around the girth and flicking her tongue over the drop of white come in the slit.

"Angel... You're killing me." He shifted his weight and dropped down onto a hip beside her.

She turned onto her side to face him, meeting his gaze and loving the way he was smiling. "I don't know why I was afraid. That was so amazing." She reached for his chest and thumbed one of his nipples.

He did the same to her before pinching the tight bud and releasing it.

She arched her chest. "I'm insatiable."

"I love it." He bent forward and suckled the swollen tip for a moment. "Give me a few minutes to catch my breath, and then you can climb over me and ride me."

Her eyes bugged out. "Seriously?"

"Yep. You can control the speed and the depth that way, but I'll warn you, I'm not sure I can keep from coming just as fast a second time." His eyes danced with happiness.

"That's okay. We can always do it a third time."

He groaned, rolled onto his back, and hauled her against his side. "Half my age..." he murmured.

She knew he was only teasing, though. He adored her, and he couldn't hide it. His adoration made her heart soar.

CHAPTER
SIXTEEN

"S hit," Addie muttered when she dropped a file folder, sending the papers flying all over the floor behind the reception desk. She'd been shaking and nervous all morning, waiting on pins and needles for Joseph to show up again.

"Adelaine Albrecht," Daddy chastised from his seat on a stool at the far end of the desk. He'd been buried in his computer for the last hour, but now he was staring at her with a narrowed gaze.

She straightened her spine, blinking at him. He'd never used her full name, not since she'd told him she preferred Addie. But the look on his face made her laugh. She couldn't stop, either. Even when she covered her mouth with her hand, giggles still erupted.

"What's so funny, naughty girl?" Bear asked as he slid off the stool and bent to pick up all the papers.

"You. You used my full name. I didn't even know you knew my last name." She cocked her head to one side as he rose with the mess of papers in hand.

After setting them on the counter, he lifted her chin with a finger. "I saw your job application sitting on the desk the day you started working. And you can expect to hear your full name from me only when you're naughty." He lifted a brow.

"What'd I do?"

He released her chin to tap her nose. "No cussing. Little girls who use naughty words get their bottoms swatted."

"Oh. Are you going to spank me?" She hoped she didn't sound too hopeful, but she'd kind of liked the spanking he'd given her the other day. He hadn't done it again. Maybe if he spanked her hard enough, he could chase away her nerves.

He searched her eyes. "Do you need me to spank you, Angel?"

"Maybe."

He gave her a slow, crooked grin before planting a quick kiss on her lips. "After work, okay?"

Her cheeks heated. It seemed strange to arrange a spanking. "Okay," she whispered.

He pulled her into his arms. "I know you're nervous, but I'm right here with you."

"Why is he still hanging around town?" she asked. She knew he was because Bear had a PI following his every move.

"I don't know, Angel. Apparently, he thinks he can still convince you to go back with him."

"But why?" She knew she was asking rhetorical questions.

"Hopefully, my PI has dug up something else interesting. I'm waiting to hear from him."

Addie tipped her head way back and set her chin on her Daddy's chest. "You know what?"

"What, Angel?"

"I don't know your name at all. Not even your first name. I assume your mother didn't name you Bear."

He chuckled. "Nope. She did not."

"So?"

He groaned. "Only one person in the club knows my name, Little one, and that's Atlas, and only because I gave him a check once."

She narrowed her gaze. "Were you sleeping with Atlas?"

He flinched as his face scrunched up. "Noooo... I can't say I've ever slept with Atlas."

"But he knows your name. You're sleeping with me, and I don't."

He tipped his head back and laughed. "Touché." He looked around, eyeing every door. She assumed he was making sure no one could hear him.

Suddenly, he picked her up by the hips and set her on the counter before crowding her with a hand on either side of her. "First of all, you have to promise never to utter it out loud to anyone, understood?"

She narrowed her gaze. "Why is it such a secret?"

"For several reasons. One is that it's a stupid name I don't use. It's my father's name, and my grandfather's before him. Secondly, it's pretentious. If it spread among my brothers, I'd never hear the end of it. Third, no one but Atlas, and now you, knows that I once bailed the club out of a financial situation. I won't keep secrets from you, Angel, but I don't want people to look at me differently."

Addie's chest tightened. He was sharing deep secrets with her. It made her realize how much she meant to him. "I would never tell a soul. I promise. Thank you for trusting me."

"You'll still call me Bear or Daddy."

"And you'll still call me Addie or Angel," she teased.

"Except when you're in trouble. If you hear your full name come out of my mouth, you can assume my palm is going to make contact with your bottom in the near future."

She squirmed at the thought. "Yes, Sir."

"My full, given, pretentious name is Edmund Maximus George III."

She winced. "Yikes. I see the problem. That is incredibly pretentious. It could only belong to someone rich."

"Exactly."

"How long have you gone by Bear?"

"Almost from the moment I arrived here and joined the club. Before I moved here, most people called me Eddie."

"You didn't even introduce yourself as Edmund or Eddie?"

"Nope. At the time, Rock's wife was still alive. She passed away several years ago, but when she first saw me, she said I looked like a Bear. It stuck. Everyone called me Bear, and no one ever asked questions."

"Oh. I wondered what happened to Remi and Atlas's mother."

"Yeah, it was sad. She was a good woman. But it's been a long time, and most of us hate that Rock hasn't met someone new. He's a wonderful guy and a great Daddy. He deserves to find someone who will spend the rest of his life with him. He's too young to give up."

Addie set her hands on Bear's chest. "You're forty-four, and you insisted you didn't want a Little girl until a few weeks ago," she reminded him.

He sighed. "How did you get so smart, Angel?"

She shrugged. "It's that useless English degree. Think how much smarter I'll be when I get my finance degree."

He chuckled. "Smarter than me. That's for sure. Did you know Atlas is an accountant?"

She shook her head.

"Yep. Until recently, he was living in the big city. The Shadowridge Guardians ran into some trouble with our treasurer. Basically, the asshole stole club money and took off. Rock asked Atlas to come home and help us get our accounting straight. Atlas reunited with Carlee, and the rest is history."

"That's so sweet. He stayed because he was in love."

"That's how it happened. Then, he opened an accounting office in town. Maybe in a few years, when you finish your degree, he'll have grown enough to need a partner."

Addie's spine went straight. The idea made her feel giddy inside. "That would be awesome."

Daddy kissed her nose. "I can't guarantee it will work out

that way, but it's certainly an option. If you let me help pay for your classes, I bet you could speed up your timetable." He lifted a brow.

She shook her head and patted his chest. "Nope. It wouldn't even help. Most of the classes I need have to be taken in order. I can't take them all at the same time. So, I'm forced to take about two a semester."

"Ah. Well, that settles that then." He lifted her off the counter and set her on her feet. "I'm going to check in with my PI."

"Okay, I'll make sense out of these papers I dropped and put the file back together."

"Holy shit."

Addie jerked her gaze toward her Daddy. He'd been on the phone for about five minutes, but he'd been mostly listening. His sudden outburst surprised her. He was shaking his head and grinning, too.

She hoped he was talking to his private investigator and that the man had found some useful information, but she couldn't imagine what it could be or why Bear would find it amusing.

Suddenly, the front door opened, and Addie stiffened as Joseph stepped into the shop.

Bear spoke again into the phone. "Thanks for the info. I've gotta call you back." He must have ended the call because he didn't say another word. He did, however, rise from his seat to stand next to Addie.

Joseph sighed as he approached. "Could I please talk to you alone, Addie?"

Bear surprised Addie when he responded before she could

manage to. "I'll tell you what, Joseph. I'll step outside and let you have a chance to talk to Addie under two conditions."

Joseph groaned. "She can make her own decisions. She doesn't need some giant bodyguard to tell her what to do."

Bear lifted a brow. "Take it or leave it."

Joseph ran a hand through his hair. "Fine. What are these conditions?"

"You stay on that side of the desk. She stays on this side. Don't even think about getting close enough to touch her."

Joseph gritted his teeth. "Fine."

"And my second condition is that you tell her all about Luke."

Joseph stiffened. If he gritted his teeth any tighter, they would crack. His face turned bright red, and he looked like he might faint.

Addie was beyond confused. Who was Luke? She didn't dare interrupt, though. Bear knew what he was doing.

"Do we have a deal?"

Joseph growled. "Yes."

Bear rounded the counter and pointed at the shop's glass front. "I'll be watching you. Don't give me a reason to come back in here. You won't like the consequences."

Joseph simply narrowed his gaze and stared at Bear as if he could take him on in a battle of wills. For the first time in her life, Addie was seeing Joseph through a new lens. He wasn't just some rich asshole who thought he could have anything he wanted, including her. He was also a wimp, especially compared to Bear. Her Daddy towered over Joseph, making him look smaller than he was.

As soon as the door closed, Addie nearly laughed. Bear stood right outside, hands on his hips, facing the two of them. She was incredibly shocked that he'd consented to this arrangement. In fact, he'd suggested it. Something his PI had told him must have caused him to find Joseph at least marginally harmless.

Joseph looked defeated as he leaned a hip against the counter, his shoulders sagging. "I had a plan," he murmured.

"Apparently. What was my role in your plan?" Addie asked, feeling stronger than she had the other day. She forced herself not to look in Bear's direction because every time she did, it was hard to keep a straight face, and she didn't want to laugh at Joseph. He was looking rather pitiful and broken.

"I figured you and I could cohabitate and come up with a mutual understanding."

"A mutual understanding?" What the hell was he talking about?

"Yeah. I knew you didn't know me well enough to have feelings for me. I did that on purpose. You're a nice enough girl. I hoped after the ceremony we could agree to pretend we were happily married but keep separate lives."

Her breath hitched. That was kind of surprising. "You didn't even want to try to get to know me and make it real?"

"No. I'm sorry, Adelaine." He winced. "Addie... I'm not interested in you like that, but I need you."

When he switched to the present tense and looked at her directly, she realized he was still hoping to win her over. "Why?"

He stood taller and faced her fully. "It would be so tidy. Think about it. I would never ask anything of you. You could do whatever you want. You'd have freedoms you've never had. I know your mother has always had you on a tight leash. I would never do that to you. Come and go as you please. Decorate our home however you want. Have friends. Take a lover. I wouldn't care."

She winced. *Take a lover?*

He sighed. "Please come home with me. If you want to write up a contract, I'll be happy to do it. We can come to an agreement."

She shook her head in confusion. "Joseph, I'm not understanding why you'd want to go to such lengths to marry someone you're not interested in. There are plenty of women in the city who have a social standing your parents would approve of. Why don't you date all of them until you find someone you love?"

He stared at her, swallowing. His face was pale, and he was breathing shallowly.

Suddenly, Addie remembered what Bear had said before he stepped outside. She glanced at her Daddy to find him watching intently, brows lifted, a slight smirk on his face. "Who's Luke?"

God, she was an idiot. She knew the answer, but she wanted Joseph to tell her himself.

"Joseph, who's Luke?" she prodded, her voice firmer.

"My boyfriend."

Even though his response had been expected, it was still startling to hear.

He ran his palm down his face. "Now you understand why I'll give you anything you want to stand by my side as my wife in name only. Please, Adelaine."

She laughed. "You can't even get my name right, Joseph."

He winced. "I'll work on it."

"I'm not going home with you, Joseph. Never. I feel pretty damn dense for not realizing you were in a relationship. That never occurred to me. But you're far denser than me if you don't realize I'm in a relationship, too."

Joseph's eyes bugged out. A few seconds ticked by before he glanced out the front window. "Are you serious? With him?" His voice rose from his shock.

Addie crossed her arms and glared at him. "Yes, with him. I'm in love with him. He treats me like spun gold, Joseph. He looks me in the eyes and talks to me about anything and everything. He opens doors, cooks for me, drives me to class, and dotes on me like I'm the most important person in the universe. I'm happy, and I wouldn't leave here for all the money in the world."

She kind of hated that she'd told Joseph she was in love with Bear before telling Bear himself. She'd rectify that soon.

Joseph drew in a deep breath. "Do you have any idea what you're giving up? Your mother will never speak to you again. She'll cut you off permanently. Hell, she'll probably leave her fortune to the pigeons at the park just to spite you."

Addie chuckled. "That's fine. I don't care. If she wants to be so stubborn that she doesn't even care about my happiness over her idea of a perfect family union, then I'll be relieved to be cut out of the family will. Life isn't all about money. There are far more important things than fancy cars, designer clothes, and luxurious, pretentious houses."

"Are there?"

She flinched. "If you don't realize that, you're not in a relationship with the right man. If you're willing to hide and lie and keep him a secret, then you must not love him like I love my man. I would never treat him like that. You might be able to trail Luke around for a while, but eventually, he'll leave you. He'll grow tired of being your sidepiece and walk away. That makes me sad for you, Joseph. You need to go home, reevaluate your priorities, and think hard about what matters to you."

Joseph continued to stare at her, but she thought he was listening. She thought she was reaching him. Finally, he blew out a breath. "You won't reconsider?"

Jesus. "No. This is my home. This is where I belong. I'm never going back to that life. I shouldn't have stayed as long as I did."

"What the hell will I tell your mother?"

"Joseph, I don't give a rat's ass what you tell my mother. Like I suggested yesterday, how about you marry her yourself? Maybe she'd agree to your terms. It's not going to be me."

"You're putting me in a tough position, Addie."

She shook her head. "I'm not putting you in any position at all. I'm following my heart. You should do the same." She rounded the desk, took long strides to the door, and opened it. She was done with this conversation. Permanently. "Goodbye, Joseph. And good luck."

He glared at her as he walked past her, and then he shifted his attention to Bear. He had to tip his head back to make eye contact. He didn't say a word, though. He simply stared as though trying to make sense of her decision before he finally turned and stomped toward his fancy rental car.

Bear stepped inside and wrapped his arms around Addie. "I love you, too, Angel. And I'm so fucking proud of you."

She gasped. "You heard me?"

"Every word. Sorry. The glass isn't that thick, and I kicked a stick into the door so it was propped open just a sliver. I figured you might have realized I would be listening when I stepped out there."

She hadn't, but she wasn't sorry. At least she didn't have to reiterate everything to Bear now that Joseph was gone. Plus, she hadn't said a single thing she wouldn't say to his face.

"How did you know about Luke?"

"My PI found him. It wasn't hard. Your ex isn't particularly careful. He meets his boyfriend most days of the week in restaurants and bars. They even have a motel they use pretty often for a few hours."

Addie winced. "I can't believe I almost married him."

"The important thing is you didn't, and now you're available to marry me instead."

She gasped. "What? We just met, and that is not a proposal."

He chuckled and pulled her closer. "Little girl, I would marry you this afternoon if you'd agree to it, but I'm also fine letting you take some time to trust that I'm never going anywhere. Not too much time, mind you, but a reasonable amount of time. One of these days, I will drop onto one knee and propose properly. I promise."

"Okay, I'm not ready for that heavy of a discussion. I'm still reeling from finding out my ex-fiancé is gay. I'm also kind of kicking myself for not noticing or paying attention. The man never paid a single bit of attention to me, not because he was an ass or didn't care but because he isn't interested in women."

"Don't beat yourself up. You dodged a bullet. Now you're free."

"I could really use that spanking about now. Do you think someone else could watch the desk and answer the phone?"

Bear chuckled. "It's a pretty damn slow afternoon. That phone hasn't rung a single time, and no one came in, which was lucky." He released her and took a step back. "I'll go talk to Kade. You go to our apartment. When I get there, I want to find you naked, face down on the bed, a pillow under your hips. Understood?"

Her pussy throbbed at his words. "Yes, Sir." She turned and practically ran for the door to the clubhouse.

"No running," Bear shouted as the door shut behind her.

She switched to a skip, giggling as she continued toward her destination.

CHAPTER
SEVENTEEN

Bear's heart was full, and he was so proud of his Little girl for standing up to her ex. She hadn't admitted it, but he knew she had to be hurting to know that her mother had no interest in maintaining a relationship with her. It was cruel, and Bear would talk to her about it. Later.

When he stepped into their bedroom and found her exactly where he'd told her to be, his cock came to full attention.

Damn, she was stunning, especially lying on her tummy with not one but two pillows under her, pushing her bottom up high.

She squirmed when he entered. She was facing him, and she smiled. "I'm ready, Daddy."

Adorable Little girl. And so obedient. "I see that. I think you deserve a reward for being such a good girl and so brave, too."

"Ice cream?" she asked, her voice teasing.

"Sure. We can get ice cream." He set his palm on her thigh and dragged it up to her pussy. She was soaked, and she pulled her knees in closer to her chest and came clear off the bed when he pushed a finger into her tight channel.

Addie moaned.

"Is ice cream what you want for a reward, Little one?" he asked as he added a second finger and rubbed her clit. He kept his attention languid. He didn't want her to come yet, but he wanted her to crave it badly.

"No, Sir," she whispered.

"Are you sure? I could let it melt and eat it off your pussy," he suggested.

She moaned.

He removed his hand and grabbed another pillow. "Spread your legs for me, Angel."

She parted her knees and whimpered when he stuffed the pillow between them. "Good girl. Keep your legs parted while I spank you."

"Daddy..." Her body was trembling. She'd never been sexier.

"Give me your hands, naughty girl. Reach them around to your back."

When she obeyed him, he wrapped his fingers around both wrists and held them together at the small of her back. "This way, you can't reach back and get your hands in the way while I'm spanking you."

Another sexy whimper as she wiggled her bottom, begging for attention with her body language.

He palmed her bottom, squeezing the globes back and forth several times before giving her a firm swat.

A deep groan filled the room. "Oh, God, Daddy... I'm going to come."

He smiled. His Little girl was so perfect. He didn't even care if she came. If spanking her made her so horny that she could come without direct contact with her pussy while he swatted her bottom, then she deserved the orgasms.

Making no response, he swatted her again. She didn't appear to need a warmup, so he peppered her bottom with a pretty firm hand, keeping a close eye on her face.

Her mouth was open, and the only thing he could read was

lust. She pulled her knees in closer to her tummy as though offering him easier access to her bottom, and he took it.

After a few minutes, she started moaning heavily. She pulled her knees in farther, curled her toes, stiffened, and cried out, "Please... Please, please, please, please."

Bear abruptly slid his hand between her legs, thrust two fingers into her pussy, and rubbed her clit.

Addie came so fast that he didn't even have a chance to order her to do so. And, fuck but she was sexy when she came. Each time he watched her orgasm, she grew more uninhibited. This time, she held nothing back, moaning and writhing while he continued to finger her.

Panting, she jerked upward so she was kneeling, spun toward him, and reached for his shirt. "Need you, Daddy." Her fingers fumbled with the front of his plaid button-down, but as soon as she managed to get a few buttons undone, she stopped and gasped.

Her wide eyes lifted to his. "You're T-shirt is pink."

He glanced down. "Is it?"

She undid a few more buttons. "I can't believe you got a pink shirt. I thought you were kidding."

"Me? Joke? Nooo..."

She giggled as she pushed his button-down off his shoulders. "Take it off, but leave it on the end of the bed. I want to wear it later."

"So bossy," he teased as he bent to remove his boots. "I suppose you want my pants off, too?"

"Daddy..."

He chuckled as he removed the rest of his clothes, grabbed a condom from the drawer, and handed it to her. He climbed up next to her and dropped onto his back.

She turned toward him. "Really? I'm in charge?"

"Angel, you're never really in charge, no. But climb on top of me and ride me. It will at least give you the illusion you're in charge."

Her hands shook as she removed the condom from the foil and reached over to roll it down his cock. "How do you know which way it goes?"

"You don't. Trial and error."

She tried it, sighed, and flipped it before unrolling it down his length. A second later, she was straddling him on her knees, his cock poised at her entrance. "I'm the luckiest Little girl alive."

He grabbed her hips and smiled. "I'm the luckiest Daddy." And he knew that to be an even more certain truth when she slowly lowered herself down his cock while tipping her head back and releasing a primal groan of satisfaction.

Bear slid his hands up to cup her fucking hot tits, molding his palms to them before pinching her pretty nipples.

"Do that again…" she begged.

He obliged, rolling them and tugging on them a few times.

Addie bounced on his cock, so very uninhibited and free. He stared at her, memorizing this moment so he could carry it with him for the rest of his life.

Two hours later, Bear stepped into the bedroom where he'd left his Little napping and frowned.

She was still asleep, which seemed excessive for late afternoon. He hated to wake her, but if he didn't, she might not be able to sleep that night.

She looked so fucking adorable, though, with his pink T-shirt on, her knees pulled up under it, and the stuffed bear hugged tightly against her chest.

As he sat on the edge of the bed, he lowered his palm to her forehead to brush away a lock of hair and winced. She felt hot. "Addie?"

She whimpered and curled into a tighter ball.

He didn't like it and immediately pulled his phone out of his pocket to text Doc. A few seconds later, he received a response that Doc was on his way.

Bear only left her long enough to open the door, and then he returned with Doc on his heels.

"What are her symptoms?" Doc asked.

"She's burning up with fever. I can't even get her to rouse. She was fine just a few hours ago, then I put her down for a nap, and when I came to check on her, I found her like this."

Doc pressed a palm on her forehead. "She is pretty hot." He set his medical bag at the foot of the bed and opened it. "Have you taken a Little girl's temperature before?"

"No. It's been a long time since I've had my own Little."

Doc pulled out a jar of lube and a thick thermometer.

Bear had heard the other Littles grumbling about having their temperatures taken from time to time, so he wasn't surprised, and he knew this was a rectal thermometer. Chances were Addie was hardly going to notice.

Doc rubbed her cheek. "Addie, can you open your eyes, Little one?"

She whimpered and shook her head. "Too tired."

"I know you are. I'm going to examine you so we can figure out what's wrong, okay?"

"Just tired," she murmured.

"I'm going to roll you onto your other side so your Daddy can take your temperature, Little one." Doc practically lifted her off the bed to rearrange her so she was facing away from them. He nodded toward the thermometer. "Open the lube, dip the tip in it, and scoop a good amount out of the jar."

Bear did as Doc instructed while Doc pushed the pink T-shirt up her back to reveal her naked bottom. He used one hand to steady her hip and the other to push her top leg toward her chest.

Bear leaned over, held his Little's bottom open, and eased the thermometer into her.

She whimpered again. "What are you doing?" It was the first lucid statement she'd made.

Doc rubbed her thigh. "Your Daddy is checking your temperature, Little one. Stay nice and still for me."

"Don't like it," she moaned.

Doc glanced at the thermometer. "You can push it a bit deeper."

Bear eased it in farther and held it.

"Daddy... Don't like it. Take it out."

"A few more minutes, Angel," he told her.

When Doc finally nodded, Bear eased it out of her and held it up. He winced when he saw that she indeed had a fever. "What do you think it could be? She was fine earlier."

Doc eased her onto her back and pulled the covers over her so her pussy wasn't exposed. "She's been under a great deal of stress lately. It's possible her body is just run down and needs the rest. A fever can be the body's way of forcing someone to relax. If she doesn't develop any other symptoms like a sore throat, runny nose, or a tummy ache, I'll be inclined to say it's stress related."

"So, what do I do?" Bear asked nervously. He hated to see his Little in pain.

"Lots of fluid and sleep. I bet she'll feel much better in a day or two. As long as she's running a fever, give her ibuprofen every four hours." He opened his bag and handed Bear a bottle of red liquid and a measuring cup. "Fill the little cup up to the line. If she's too asleep to rouse, use a dropper to get her to swallow it."

"Okay."

Doc rose from the bed. "I saw King in the kitchen on my way by. I'll ask if he can bring you some apple juice. He likes to have something to do and feel useful on his days off." Doc smiled.

"Thank you." Bear didn't want to leave Addie even for a moment. What if she needed him or rolled off the side of the bed?

Doc cleaned the thermometer with a disinfectant wipe and set it and the lube on the nightstand. "I'll leave this here so you can check again in a while. Text me if anything changes." He zipped up his bag and clapped Bear on the shoulder. "She'll be fine. Littles get sick sometimes. The hardest thing is convincing them to stay in bed."

Bear nodded.

"I'll let myself out."

As soon as Doc was gone, Bear rearranged the covers and tucked her stuffie in her arms. "Let's get some medicine in you, Angel." He filled the measuring cup, cupped the back of her head, and lifted her a few inches. "Can you swallow this for Daddy?"

She opened her mouth and let him pour it in, thank goodness. "Mmm. Yummy."

That was a relief. At least she liked it.

"Knock, knock."

At the sound of King's voice, Bear twisted his head around. "Come in."

King stepped into the bedroom, holding out a sippy cup. "I heard you have a sick Little girl on your hands."

"Yes. Thank you for bringing us some juice."

"I fixed three sippy cups. I'll stick the other two in your fridge. Let me know if I can help out any other way."

"Can you let Kade know she won't be at work tomorrow?"

"Of course."

"And Eden. She'll be worried."

"No problem." King patted the side of the bed. "Hope she feels better soon."

Me, too. For the first time since Bear had realized Addie was his, he felt nervous and helpless. Sure, he was a big guy, and everyone thought he was rough around the edges, but he couldn't stand to see a Little suffer. That feeling was tenfold now that it was his own Little.

He climbed onto the bed, lowered onto his side facing her, and slid his arm under her head. "Drink some juice for me, Angel," he encouraged, holding the sippy cup to her lips.

Addie whimpered, but she took several drinks before pushing the cup away. "Tired, Daddy."

He kissed her temple. "Okay, Little one. Rest now. Daddy will be right here."

CHAPTER
EIGHTEEN

"Daddy?"

Bear jumped up from the couch and rushed into the bedroom to find Addie pushing herself up to sit. It had been two days since she'd come down with a fever, and she'd nearly had him pulling his hair out.

It was a relief to find her looking right at him with clarity in her eyes. Thank goodness her fever had finally broken.

She licked her lips. "Thirsty."

He sat on the edge of the bed and handed her the sippy cup from the nightstand. "You look much better, Angel. How do you feel?"

"Better," she answered after she took a long drink. She was shaking, which was understandable after sleeping so much.

"I bet you're hungry. You've only had broth and juice for two days."

She nodded. "Can you make me pancakes?"

He smiled. It was a good sign that she wanted pancakes. "I'd love to, Angel. Do you think you'll be okay here for a few minutes while I do that?"

She nodded.

He helped her scoot back against the headboard. "No getting up, understood?"

"Yes, Sir."

The other Littles had all gathered and made her a basket of things to do while she was on bed rest, but she hadn't been able to do anything yet. He was finally able to present it to her, so he grabbed it from the floor and set it on the bed before pulling out a brand-new coloring book and a box of crayons. He even set a lap desk on her thighs.

She pulled the crayons up to her chest and hugged them. "I'm going to use them until they are nothing but tiny stubs, and I'm going to mix them all up in the box with no rhyme or reason," she declared.

He smiled and kissed her forehead. "That's the idea." He pointed at the basket. "When you get tired of coloring, there's a Barbie in there that looks just like you, and Eden bought you a pink dress so you could change her clothes."

Tears welled up in Addie's eyes, and she swiped them away. "Thank you," she whispered.

"You're welcome, Angel. I'll be right back with pancakes." Bear hated leaving her, but he wanted to fix her the pancakes she desired, so he hurried to the main kitchen and fixed a batch as fast as he could.

In no time, he was back at her side with a tray of food. "I made you scrambled eggs, too. You need some protein."

"Thank you, Daddy. That smells so good." She set her coloring book aside and held up a picture. "Look what I colored." It was a picture of a bear, and she'd added a pink T-shirt to it.

He chuckled. "I love it. I'll hang it on the fridge."

He sat next to her and let her eat in peace, rubbing her legs the entire time.

"This is delicious, Daddy. Much better than the cold ones I ate the day I met you."

He chuckled. "They are better warm."

When she finished eating, he set the tray on the floor and returned to his spot. He needed to tell her something, and he hoped she wouldn't be too upset, especially with him.

"Angel, you got a few texts while you were feverish, and I read them because I was concerned about you not being able to respond in case they were from one of your professors or someone important."

She cocked her head to one side. "Oh no! My classes!"

"Don't worry. You only missed one algebra class. Eden let the professor know you were sick, and she brought you the homework assignment. I'm sure you can get caught up in no time."

Addie relaxed. "Oh good." Then she frowned. "What were the texts about then?"

"They were from Joseph. He must have gotten your number from his PI. It wouldn't have been difficult."

Addie winced and rolled her eyes. "Oh, great. Can't he just leave me alone?"

"Apparently not. In the first one, he said your mother was livid that you hadn't returned with him. She told him to let you know that you would not be welcome back in her life if you didn't return immediately and do the right thing." Bear drew in a breath as he watched Addie's reaction.

Luckily, she rolled her eyes. "Good. Hopefully, she'll make good on that promise." Her bottom lip quivered as she finished speaking, and her eyes welled up with tears.

Bear slid his arms under his Little girl and lifted her to pull her onto his lap. He leaned her close to his chest and cradled her head against his shoulder. "I'm so sorry, Addie. No matter what, I know it hurts. She's your mother. No one should be shunned like that by their own parent."

Addie started crying, which was probably for the best. She needed to let herself mourn; otherwise, she wouldn't be able to move forward.

Bear's heart hurt as he rubbed her back and rocked her.

"Let it all out, Angel. I know there's a lot of emotions inside you. Daddy's got you."

She cried for a long time before finally reducing to hiccups and sniffles. She was going to be exhausted. He hated having to drop that on her lap at the tail end of her illness. Hopefully, she wouldn't regress.

He wiped her nose and eyes with a tissue before offering her the sippy cup. After taking a long drink, she leaned back and looked at him. Her eyes were bloodshot and swollen. "You said there were two texts. What was the other one?"

Bear smiled. "It was long, but basically, Joseph said after watching both his parents and your mom behave like the world had come to an end over your disappearance, he'd taken your advice and told his parents about Luke. He isn't sure what will happen next, but he left them stunned and is going to follow his heart."

Addie's small smile grew wide. "Good for him."

"I thought you'd like that part. When you're feeling better in a few days, maybe you should text him back and wish him luck."

"I'll do that. Thank you, Daddy." She wrapped her arms around his neck and hugged him tight. "I'm so glad I have you."

"I'm so glad I have you, too, Little one. Now, don't get sick like that on me again. I nearly pulled out all my hair worrying."

She giggled. "I'll do my best."

CHAPTER
NINETEEN

F*ive days later...*

Addie was so excited. Today, her Daddy and Doc had finally cleared her to resume all regular activities. Her week in bed had been fun, considering how many toys and games her Daddy had pampered her with, but she'd grown antsy and had wanted to get up and get back to her life.

Although she had missed several classes, she had kept up with her assignments, communicated regularly with her two professors, and felt confident she was on track.

Tonight, Daddy was finally letting her join the other Littles in the common room for a movie night. He'd even made popcorn and hot chocolate to make up for the first night she'd joined the Littles when they'd all gotten into trouble and missed out on the snacks.

The Littles had piled up dozens of pillows and blankets in front of the giant television, and they all sat in a circle, sipping hot cocoa while Bear and several of the other Daddies set up the movie they had requested.

"I'm kind of picturing a popcorn fight," Elizabeth whispered.

Talon turned from the television, stomped over to the Littles, set his hand on his hips, and gave them all a narrow-eyed glare. "No popcorn fights."

Elizabeth gave a fake groan. "You're no fun."

"I mean it. Any of that popcorn that isn't in the bowls or your tummies after the movie will be picked up by your toes one kernel at a time until every last piece is in the trashcan."

Addie fought the urge to giggle at the visual.

Elizabeth flopped onto her side dramatically. "Daddy, that would take forever. Our toes?"

Bear joined him. "That's an excellent punishment. No hands. You girls can waddle around in here, picking up each piece with your toes until it's all cleaned up. Still want to have a popcorn fight?"

Addie shook her head. That sounded awful.

The other Littles shook their heads in agreement.

"Good," Talon growled. "Now, if you need a round of spankings, we'll be happy to deliver after the movie is finished. I propose you whine when we tell you to go to bed. That's a much better way to get what you need. The popcorn idea is terrible."

Addie glanced at Eden to find all the Littles looking around at each other. They all nodded in agreement.

Eden licked her lips and spoke for the group. "We can whine."

Addie started giggling so hard she nearly dumped her bucket of popcorn by accident. What a life she lived. She suddenly had a gigantic family filled with so much love and happiness.

When she'd been young, she'd had good times with her

father, and she would always remember him fondly and miss him, but apparently, her mother wished to remain estranged. If her heart was so cold that she couldn't accept her daughter for who she was, Addie had to find a way to live her life without wasting time thinking about the bitter woman.

She tipped her head back and found her Daddy smiling down at her. Yeah, this was where she belonged. These were her people. Her family. *I love you,* she mouthed at him.

He smiled broadly and mouthed back, *I love you, too, Angel.*

As soon as the Littles were all comfortable and ready for the movie to start, the door to the common room opened, and Faust stepped in.

Addie gasped. So did the others.

Faust was scowling as he glanced around. He had a black eye, and his knuckles were bloody as though he'd been in a fight. From Addie's perspective, she assumed he'd probably won the fight, but he'd also taken a few hard hits.

"What happened?" Steele asked.

"Don't want to talk about it," Faust growled before he stomped through the common room and down the hall.

Steele sighed. "That man is going to need to get a grip on his temper, or it's going to bite him in the ass one of these days."

Bear came to Addie's side, leaned over, and kissed the top of her head.

She tipped her head back. "Will he be okay?"

"Yeah. He's hot-headed. This isn't unusual for him. He'll be fine."

Bear leaned closer, tipped her head back, and kissed her lips. "Love you," he repeated, bringing her back into her warm and happy place.

"Love you, too, Daddy."

"Enjoy your movie. I'll spank you afterward if you need it," he teased.

She squirmed as she settled in while someone turned the lights off. Daddy hadn't spanked her in over a week, not since before she'd gotten sick. She was kind of craving that sort of attention. While the movie started, she mentally worked on the perfect whiny voice.

Being Little was so much fun.

AUTHOR'S NOTE

I hope you're enjoying the Shadowridge Guardians MC series as much as we are enjoying writing them! The next book in the series is Faust by Pepper North.

Shadowridge Guardians MC
Steele by Pepper North
Kade by Kate Oliver
Atlas by Becca Jameson
Doc by Kate Oliver
Gabriel by Becca Jameson
Talon by Pepper North
Bear by Becca Jameson
Faust by Pepper North
Storm by Kate Oliver

Combining the sizzling talents of bestselling authors Pepper North, Kate Oliver, and Becca Jameson, the Shadowridge Guardians are guaranteed to give you a thrill and leave you dreaming of your own throbbing motorcycle joyride.

Are you daring enough to ride with a club of rough, growly,

commanding men? The protective Daddies of the Shadowridge Guardians Motorcycle Club will stop at nothing to ensure the safety and protection of everything that belongs to them: their Littles, their club, and their town. Throw in some sassy, naughty, mischievous women who won't hesitate to serve their fair share of attitude even in the face of looming danger, and this brand new MC Romance series is ready to ignite!

ALSO BY BECCA JAMESON

Seattle Doms:

Salacious Exposure by Becca Jameson

Salacious Desires By Kate Oliver

Salacious Attraction by Becca Jameson

Salacious Indulgence by Kate Oliver

Salacious Devotion by Becca Jameson

Salacious Surrender by Kate Oliver

Danger Bluff:

Rocco

Hawking

Kestrel

Magnus

Phoenix

Caesar

Roses and Thorns:

Marigold

Oleander

Jasmine

Tulip

Daffodil

Lily

Bite of Pain Anthology: Gemma's Release

Shadowridge Guardians:

Steele by Pepper North

Kade by Kate Oliver

Atlas by Becca Jameson

Doc by Kate Oliver

Gabriel by Becca Jameson

Talon by Pepper North

Bear by Becca Jameson

Faust by Pepper North

Storm by Kate Oliver

Blade by Pepper North

King by Kate Oliver

Rock by Becca Jameson

Blossom Ridge:

Starting Over

Finding Peace

Building Trust

Feeling Brave

Embracing Joy

Accepting Love

Blossom Ridge Box Set One

Blossom Ridge Box Set Two

The Wanderers:

Sanctuary

Refuge

Harbor

Shelter

Hideout

Haven

The Wanderers Box Set One

The Wanderers Box Set Two

Surrender:

Raising Lucy

Teaching Abby

Leaving Roman

Choosing Kellen

Pleasing Josie

Honoring Hudson

Nurturing Britney

Charming Colton

Convincing Leah

Rewarding Avery

Impressing Brett

Guiding Cassandra

Chasing Amber

Controlling Natasha

Provoking Camden

Surrender Box Set One

Surrender Box Set Two

Surrender Box Set Three

Open Skies:

Layover

Redeye

Nonstop

Standby

Takeoff

Jetway

Open Skies Box Set One

Open Skies Box Set Two

Shadow SEALs:

Shadow in the Desert

Shadow in the Darkness

Holt Agency:

Rescued by Becca Jameson

Unchained by KaLyn Cooper

Protected by Becca Jameson

Liberated by KaLyn Cooper

Defended by Becca Jameson

Unrestrained by KaLyn Cooper

Delta Team Three (Special Forces: Operation Alpha):

Destiny's Delta

Canyon Springs:

Caleb's Mate

Hunter's Mate

Corked and Tapped:

Volume One: Friday Night

Volume Two: Company Party

Volume Three: The Holidays

Project DEEP:

Reviving Emily

Reviving Trish

Reviving Dade

Reviving Zeke

Reviving Graham

Reviving Bianca

Reviving Olivia

Project DEEP Box Set One

Project DEEP Box Set Two

SEALs in Paradise:

Hot SEAL, Red Wine

Hot SEAL, Australian Nights

Hot SEAL, Cold Feet

Hot SEAL, April's Fool

Hot SEAL, Brown-Eyed Girl

Dark Falls:

Dark Nightmares

Club Zodiac:

Training Sasha

Obeying Rowen

Collaring Brooke

Mastering Rayne

Trusting Aaron

Claiming London

Sharing Charlotte

Taming Rex

Tempting Elizabeth

Club Zodiac Box Set One

Club Zodiac Box Set Two

Club Zodiac Box Set Three

The Art of Kink:

Pose

Paint

Sculpt

Arcadian Bears:

Grizzly Mountain

Grizzly Beginning

Grizzly Secret

Grizzly Promise

Grizzly Survival

Grizzly Perfection

Arcadian Bears Box Set One

Arcadian Bears Box Set Two

Sleeper SEALs:

Saving Zola

Spring Training:

Catching Zia

Catching Lily

Catching Ava

Spring Training Box Set

The Underground series:

Force

Clinch

Guard

Submit

Thrust

Torque

The Underground Box Set One

The Underground Box Set Two

Wolf Masters series:

Kara's Wolves

Lindsey's Wolves

Jessica's Wolves

Alyssa's Wolves

Tessa's Wolf

Rebecca's Wolves

Melinda's Wolves

Laurie's Wolves

Amanda's Wolves

Sharon's Wolves

Wolf Masters Box Set One

Wolf Masters Box Set Two

Claiming Her series:

The Rules

The Game

The Prize

Claiming Her Box Set

Emergence series:

Bound to be Taken

Bound to be Tamed

Bound to be Tested

Bound to be Tempted

Emergence Box Set

The Fight Club series:

Come

Perv

Need

Hers

Want

Lust

The Fight Club Box Set One

The Fight Club Box Set Two

Wolf Gatherings series:

Tarnished

Dominated

Completed

Redeemed

Abandoned

Betrayed

Wolf Gatherings Box Set One

Wolf Gathering Box Set Two

Durham Wolves series:

Rescue in the Smokies

Fire in the Smokies

Freedom in the Smokies

Durham Wolves Box Set

Stand Alone Books:

Blind with Love

Guarding the Truth

Out of the Smoke

Abducting His Mate

Wolf Trinity

Frostbitten

A Princess for Cale / A Princess for Cain

Severed Dreams

Where Alphas Dominate

ABOUT THE AUTHOR

Becca Jameson is a USA Today best-selling author of over 150 books. She is well-known for her Wolf Masters series, her Fight Club series, and her Surrender series. She currently lives in Houston, Texas, with her husband. Two grown kids pop in every once in a while, too! She is loving this journey and has dabbled in a variety of genres, including paranormal, sports romance, military, reverse harem, dark romance, suspense, dystopian, BDSM, and Daddy Dom.

A total night owl, Becca writes late at night, sequestering herself in her office with a glass of red wine and a bar of dark chocolate, her fingers flying across the keyboard as her characters weave their own stories.

During the day--which never starts before ten in the morning!--she can be found walking, running errands, or reading in her favorite hammock chair!

…where Alphas dominate…

Becca's Newsletter Sign-up

Join my Facebook fan group, Becca's Bibliomaniacs, for the most up-to-date information, random excerpts while I work, giveaways, and fun release parties!

Facebook Fan Group:
Becca's Bibliomaniacs

Contact Becca:
www.beccajameson.com
beccajameson4@aol.com

facebook.com/becca.jameson.18
x.com/beccajameson
instagram.com/becca.jameson
bookbub.com/authors/becca-jameson
goodreads.com/beccajameson
amazon.com/author/beccajameson

Printed in Great Britain
by Amazon